Also by Lucy Ellis

Innocent in the Ivory Tower
Untouched by His Diamonds
The Man She Shouldn't Crave
Pride After Her Fall
A Dangerous Solace
Caught in His Gilded World
Kept at the Argentine's Command

Discover more at millsandboon.co.uk

REDEMPTION OF A RUTHLESS BILLIONAIRE

BY
LUCY ELLIS

MILLS & BOON

First Published in Great Britain 2018
by Mills & Boon, an imprint of HarperCollins*Publishers*
1 London Bridge Street, London, SE1 9GF

© 2018 Lucy Ellis

ISBN: 978-0-263-93410-6

MIX
Paper from
responsible sources
FSC® C007454

This book is produced from independently certified FSC™ paper
to ensure responsible forest management.
For more information visit www.harpercollins.co.uk/green.

Printed and bound in Spain
by CPI, Barcelona

To the memory of my dear dad—Robert 'Jim' Giblett—
who didn't get to see this one finished after many hours
on the phone listening to me making up these stories,
laughing in the right places and telling me I could do it
when I thought I couldn't.

Life isn't the same without you, Dad.
You were everything to me, your Lucy/Kareena.

CHAPTER ONE

'I'VE FOUND YOU a girl,' was the unexpected news his grandfather greeted Nik Voronov with cheerfully. 'She's local, so you'll have to come down.'

The key words, Nik suspected, were, *You'll have to come down.*

His conscience pricked. He hadn't set out ten years ago, when he'd founded his company, to work twelve-hour days and seven-day weeks, but he did. He had the world on his shoulders, and his grandfather more of late on his conscience, and balancing the two was hard.

Nik lowered his head as a gust of wind buffeted him on the approach to the complex of site buildings where he had an office.

Around him was the site where his company, Voroncor, were sinking down exploratory equipment and mining kimberlite deposits from the rich Siberian earth. Work went on all year round, and because it was January everything was white except in patches where the ashy black earth showed through.

At least the wind had died down and he could see what he was looking at. Three years' hard work to pull this reserve into the Voroncor fold.

'Is that right, Deda?'

'Her name is Sybella and she has everything a man could want. She cooks and cleans and she's wonderful with children!'

The triumvirate of qualities guaranteed to ensure a man a good life, according to his seventy-nine-year-old grandfather.

Nik was well aware he could remind the old man he had

a chef on the payroll, cleaning staff for all four of his international residences and no children to speak of. Moreover, no woman in the twenty-first century would view cooking, cleaning and raising children her sole responsibility.

But he'd be wasting his breath and it wasn't the point.

Tactfully he rolled out the line he'd been using since his grandfather became actively interested in his personal life, which had—not mysteriously—coincided with the loss of his own wife, Nik's adored grandmother.

'When and if I do meet the right woman, you'll be the first to know, Deda.'

His grandfather harrumphed. 'I've seen you on the Internet with that model.'

The Internet? The last time they'd spoken the old man was using the tablet he'd got him as a tea tray.

But he knew who his grandfather was referring to.

Voroncor's sister company Voroncor Holdings had bought out a retail corporation and Nik found himself in possession of some premium retail brands, including the fashion house Spanish model/actress and 'it' girl Marla Mendez was currently spruiking for.

The lady had pursued him around the world seeking his investment in her personal project, a lingerie line, not exactly his field but he had a personal reason for stumping up the funds that had nothing to do with Ms Mendez herself. A few photographs of them together at events had been enough for the tabloids to seize on the idea they were personally involved. He saw no reason to set his grandfather straight.

'That woman is not right for you, Nikolka. There is something hard about her. She would not be good with little children.'

Nik considered reminding his grandfather he had no children, but he suspected that was Deda's point.

'Sybella works with children,' his grandfather added helpfully.

No surprises there.

'I think you should come and see her at work. I think you would be impressed, *moy mal'chik*.'

There was a long pause as Nik shouldered his way down the corridor and into his office, signalling for a coffee as he passed one of his admin assistants.

'Did you hear me, Nikolka?'

'I'm here, Deda. How did you meet her?'

Nik began pulling off his gloves, idly glancing at the information he'd asked for on the screen of a laptop another assistant silently opened in front of him.

'She lives down the lane from the Hall, in the village. She's a tenant. I believe she pays you rent.'

Vaguely Nik remembered some old English custom of the squire having first rights to local virgins. He held fire on mentioning it to his grandfather.

When he'd bought Edbury Hall a year ago he'd flown over in a helicopter. The village below had been merely a small sea of roofs swallowed up by the encroaching forest. His attention had been on the magnificent Elizabethan 'E', its outbuildings and the undulating pastureland around it.

His lawyer had done the groundwork and put everything in place. The purchase was a good investment, and it currently housed his grandfather while he was in the UK undergoing tests and treatment for a variety of complaints set off by his diabetes.

Nik hadn't paid much attention to a lane, or the village, or the fact he had tenants. His admin dealt with that.

'What are you doing consorting with the tenants? That's not your problem, Deda. You're supposed to be relaxing.'

'Sybella comes to the house to keep me company and help me out with a few secretarial things.'

'You have staff for that.'

'I prefer Sybella. She is genuine.'

'She sounds great,' Nik said mildly enough, making a mental note to ask a few questions of the house staff. He didn't want his grandfather's kindly nature being taken advantage of.

'We have a busload of children from all over the county once a month, up to thirty at a time, and Sybella is unflappable.'

'Unflappable, good to know.' Nik indicated he had what he needed. Then his head shot up. 'Busloads of—what? Hang on, Deda, where is this?'

'At the Hall. The children who come to see the house.'

Nik stopped finding this amusing. 'Why are busloads of children coming to the house?' But he already knew.

'The Heritage Trust show them around,' Deda said cheerfully.

The Heritage Trust. The local historic buildings preservation group, who had kept the Hall open to the public since the nineteen seventies.

His purchase a year ago had shut all commercial activities at the Hall down. There had been a picket at the end of the drive for a week in protest until he'd called in the police.

'This is not what we agreed, Deda.'

'I know what you're about to say,' his grandfather blustered, 'but I changed my mind. Besides, no final decision was made.'

'No, we talked about it when you moved in and we decided to leave the matter in my hands.'

'And now it's in Sybella's,' his grandfather said smugly. Sybella.

Nik couldn't help picturing one of the matronly women who had picketed the drive, in her husband's oversized hunting jacket and wellington boots, face like the back of a shovel, shouting about British heritage and marching a troop of equally appalling kids through his grandfather's home. When she wasn't going through Deda's papers and possibly siphoning his bank account.

This was not what he wanted to hear. He had a new pipe starting up in Archangelsk, which would keep him in the north for much of this year. Business was expanding and he needed to be on site.

But now he had a new problem: a white elephant of a property sitting up in the English Cotswolds he'd been ignoring for too long, currently housing his grandfather and apparently the local historical group.

Nik didn't have time for this, but he knew he was going to have to make time.

'And what does this *Sybella* have to do with the Heritage Trust when she's not cooking and cleaning and herding children?' he asked tightly.

His grandfather chuckled and delivered the coup de grâce. 'She runs it.'

CHAPTER TWO

THE PRESIDENT OF the local branch of the Heritage Trust stood up, removed her glasses and announced somewhat dolefully to the committee members assembled that a legal document had been lodged this morning at the trust's London office suspending any further activity of the trust in the Hall.

'Does that mean we can't use the empty gatehouse as a visitors' centre?' Mrs Merrywether wanted to know. 'Because Sybella said we could.'

A dozen grey heads turned and Sybella found herself sinking a little lower in her chair, because she had indeed waved a letter around last month claiming they had the right.

But dodging responsibility wasn't her way.

'I can't understand why this has happened,' she told the meeting, feeling very guilty and responsible for the confusion that had gripped the room. 'I'll look into it and sort it out. I promise.'

Seated beside her Mr Williams, the retired local accountant, patted her arm. 'We know you will, Sybella, we trust your judgement. You haven't led us wrong once.'

There was a hum of agreement, which only made Sybella feel worse as she packed up her notes and made her usual early departure.

She had worked hard for twelve months to make Edbury Hall a place of life and activity for its new incumbent, Mr Voronov, and continue to earn its keep for the village. While this house might personally remind her of some grim stage set for a horror film starring Christopher

Lee, the Hall also brought in its share of the tourist trade and kept the local shops turning over.

If this all collapsed it would affect everybody. And she would be responsible.

Rugging herself up in the boot room for her dash home, Sybella fished her phone out of her jeans back pocket and rang her sister-in-law.

Meg lived in a jaunty little semi-detached house on a busy road in Oxford, where she taught art to people with no real aptitude for painting and belly danced at a local Egyptian restaurant. She took off and travelled at the drop of a hat. Her life was possibly the one Sybella would have gravitated towards if life in all its infinite twists of fate hadn't set her on another course, with much more responsibility and less room to move. Sybella considered Meg her best friend.

'It's the letters. I should have known,' she groaned after a brief rundown on tonight's meeting. 'Nobody writes letters any more.'

'Unless you're a lonely seventy-nine-year-old man rattling around in a big empty house, trying to fill it with people,' said Meg.

Sybella sighed. Every time something new occurred at the Hall Mr Voronov gave the same advice.

*Just write to my grandson and let him know. I'm sure there will be no problems.'

So she had. She'd written just as she'd been writing every month for the past year detailing events at Edbury Hall.

Because she'd been too damn timid to face him on the phone.

She'd let her native shyness trip her up—again—and this was the tip, Sybella suspected, of a huge iceberg that was going to take her little ship out. She said as much, leaving out the bit about being a timid mouse. Meg didn't cut you slack for being a mouse.

'My ship, Meg. My ship of fools, me being the captain!'

Meg was silent and Sybella already knew what was coming.

'You know what this is a result of? That weird life you lead in the village.'

'Please, Meg, not now.' Sybella shouldered her way out of the boot room. The corridor was dark and faintly menacing, although she suspected anyone coming across her would probably run the other way. She was wearing her Climb and Ski gear that was packed with a substance that was supposed to keep you warm and dry in the Arctic. It wasn't particularly flattering to a woman's figure and it also inhibited natural movement. She was aware she currently resembled a yeti.

Meg was persistent. 'You hang around with all those oldies…'

'You know why I volunteer with the Heritage Trust. It's going to get me a job in the end.'

Sybella made her way to the servants' entrance, from which she could slip unnoticed out of the house, cross the courtyard and disappear through a space in the hedge that led to the lane that wound down the hill to the top of her road.

'Really? You've been doing unpaid work for them for over a year. When does it pay off for you?'

'It's work experience in my field. Do you know how difficult it is to get a job with just a degree?'

'I don't know why you won't move down to Oxford with me. It's bristling with opportunities.'

'Your parents are here,' she said firmly. She was always firm when it came to her daughter's well-being. 'And I'm not removing Fleur from her home.'

'It's a two-hour drive. They can see her on weekends.'

'Who is going to look after her while I'm at work? Think of the practicalities, Meg.' God knew she had to. If she hadn't been so busy juggling all the balls life had thrown at her she might have thought through those practicalities with a little more precision at the Hall.

'Fair enough,' conceded Meg. 'But you've put a lot of eggs in that house of horrors basket.'

'Yes, because I have a growing daughter who has her roots in this village—a village with no other job opportunities in my chosen field. I've tried Stansfield Castle, Belfort Castle and Lark House. None are interested in someone with lots of education but no on-the-ground experience. Without Edbury Hall, Meg, I'm stuck!'

'So in the meantime you're writing letters to a man you're never going to meet. Should I ask about your love life?'

'What has my love life got to do with the letters?'

'I think if you had a boyfriend you wouldn't have all this extra time to sit around writing letters and sealing envelopes. You'd be like the rest of us and use freaking email.'

'It wasn't extra time. It was extra *effort*. Besides, I do use email. And I'm not looking for a romantic relationship, Meg Parminter.'

'I don't know why not. My brother's been gone six years. You can't keep hiding away in Mouldering Manor with those oldies, Syb. Seize the day!'

Given her days were quite long, what with her part-time archivist job at the town hall, her volunteer work with the Heritage Trust and sole responsibility for her home-schooled five-year-old daughter, Sybella wasn't quite sure which part of the day she wasn't seizing.

Besides, the idea of taking off her clothes in front of a man after six years of not having to endure that specific kind of embarrassment with Simon was not an encouraging one.

'You know that film you love, *The Ghost and Mrs. Muir*?' Meg asked. 'Do you remember at the end when her daughter comes home all grown up with the fiancé? One day that will be Fleur, feeling guilty because she's got a life and you haven't!'

'I will have a life,' Sybella shot back, confident at least on this point. 'I'll be in the midst of a brilliant career as a curator and very fulfilled in my life's ambition, thank you very much.'

'Okay, maybe that analogy doesn't work in the twenty-first century,' Meg grudgingly allowed. 'But are you really going to wait another twenty years before you pull the "take a detour" sign down off your bed?'

Sybella pushed open the heavy wooden door and made her way outside. She blew out a breath and watched it take shape in the air.

Blast, it was cold.

'It's not a priority for me, Meg.'

'Well, it should be!'

Sybella looked around to make sure no one was lurking in the bushes to overhear this.

'I really don't want to discuss my sex life, or lack of. I'm just not interested,' she said firmly. 'There, I've said it. Not. Interested. In. Sex. I am, however, very interested in what I'm going to say to Mr Voronov's grandson when he prosecutes us!'

Which was when she noticed a pricey-looking off-road vehicle coming up the drive, followed by another and another.

Mr Voronov hadn't mentioned guests. She was familiar with his schedule, given she came and gave him a hand with a few things he refused to entrust to the personal assistant his grandson had engaged for him.

She told Meg she'd call her tomorrow and stowed her phone, pulled the ski mask down over her chin to repel the cold and headed out across the drive to see what they wanted.

Nik parked in the courtyard, slammed the door behind him and crunched through the snow to open the boot and retrieve his overnight bag.

He'd never seen England's little tourist Mecca from this vantage point. Driving in, he thought it looked very much as if he'd stumbled onto the film set of the dramatisation of an Agatha Christie novel. Or maybe it was a recreation of Shakespeare's youth because if he wasn't mistaken, as the road had opened out into the town square, there had been a maypole.

Sticking up like a needle without a thread.

Everything else was under a ton of snow and ice.

He glanced up at the looming walls of Edbury Hall, with its multifaceted windows and grey stone. Snow drifts had made clumps of the carefully tended hedges and topiary.

It was a picture postcard of Ye Olde England.

No wonder those crackpots and loonies from Edbury's branch of the Heritage Trust were bombarding his offices in London every time something got raised or lowered on the property.

He sensed rather than heard movement coming up behind him.

Good. Someone around this place was doing their job.

'Here.' He bundled the luggage at the rugged-up figure hovering at his shoulder. Then he slammed the back of the vehicle closed and hit the lock device on his keys.

He turned around to find the help was staggering under its weight. Which didn't last long because the next thing he knew the guy was lying flat on his back in the snow.

He waited. The man wasn't getting up. He did, however, stick a gloved hand in the air and wave it around. He also made a noise that sounded like a cat being drowned in a barrel. Nik liked animals; he didn't much like incompetence in people.

Which was when he noticed the black ski mask under the hood of the guy's coat and Nik lost his easy stance, because in Russia personal security was often a matter of life and death, and right now instinct was telling him this guy was not one of the people he had authorised to work for his grandfather.

He grabbed the interloper by the scruff of his coat and heaved him to his feet.

Sybella tried to cry out but her voice box was currently lodged somewhere in the snow after the impact of hitting the ground.

She found herself being lifted by the scruff of her neck until she was almost hanging, her parka cutting up under her arms, the toes of her new boots scrambling for purchase.

'Give me your name and your reason for being out here.'

Her assailant had a deep, growly baritone that corresponded with his size. His rich Russian accent meant he probably had something to do with the current owner of this property. Given his size and strength he was possibly a bodyguard.

He was also clearly a bear.

'*Imya?*' he barked out when she didn't immediately respond.

'There's been a mistake,' Sybella gasped through the fine wool barrier formed by the ski mask over her mouth.

'What are you, journalist, protester, what?' He gave her another shake. 'I'm losing patience.'

'Put me down,' she pleaded. 'I don't understand what's happening.'

But even to her ears her plea was muffled into incoherence by all the wool and the wind.

Nevertheless, he dropped her and she landed heavily on the soles of her boots. Before she could react he whipped back the hood of her parka and gathered up a handful of her ski mask, yanking on her hair in the process. The ski mask came away and with it her long heavy flaxen curls. Freed, they began whipping around her face in the frigid wind.

His arms dropped to his sides.

'You're a woman,' he said in English as if this was entirely improbable. His voice was deep and firm and weirdly—given the circumstances—reassuring.

Sybella pushed the wildly flapping hair from her eyes and, finally able to be understood, choked out a little desperately, 'I was the last time I looked!'

He stepped in front of her, and if she didn't suspect a little brain damage from all the pushing and shoving, she'd think it was to shield her from the wind and elements.

'Did I hurt you?' he demanded, his head bent to hers.

'N-no.' Scared the life out of her, but she was in one piece.

At least she no longer felt in danger of ending up on her bottom again. She was also staring, because you didn't see men like this every day in Edbury.

He was a good head taller than her and she couldn't see around his shoulders and up close he had slightly slanted grey eyes, thick golden lashes, high flat cheekbones and a strong jaw stubbled in gold. He was gorgeous. His mouth was wide and firm and she found her attention constantly returning to it.

'What are you doing out here?' he demanded.

She could have asked him the same question.

Trying to gather her wits, Sybella took her time checking the seams on the arms of her parka. They appeared intact. Seams, that was. Apparently the fabric could withstand being dangled by a bear, but not the ingress of water. She was soaked through.

And cold.

'I asked you a question,' he repeated. He really was very rude.

'Minding my own business,' she said pointedly, making a show of brushing the snow off her cords to cover the fact her hands were shaking.

'Never show them you're rattled' was one of the few useful lessons a draconian English public boarding school education had taught her. Also, 'be the one asking the questions'—it made you look as if you knew what you were doing.

'Maybe the better question is what are you doing here?' Pity her voice shook a bit.

'I own this house.'

Her head shot up. 'No, you don't. Mr Voronov does.'

'I am Voronov,' he said. 'Nikolai Aleksandrovich Voronov. You are talking about my grandfather.'

Sybella's knees turned to jelly and a funny buzzing sound began to ring in her ears.

'Kolya?' she said a little faintly.

His eyes narrowed and Sybella felt as if she'd been knocked over in the snow for the second time tonight. Somehow, some way, she'd got this all wrong.

He looked her up and down.

'Who did you say you were?'

CHAPTER THREE

IN TROUBLE, THAT was who she was.

'I asked you a question,' he repeated.

Yes, he had, and he expected an answer, she interpreted from the way he just stood there, arms folded, on closer inspection less like a bear and more like some angry Norse god.

'Speak,' he commanded.

She literally jumped but then her training kicked in. She handled tour groups of small children regularly and knew one had to establish rules and boundaries if chaos wasn't to ensue.

'I think you need to calm down,' she said shakily, aware her heart was beating so fast she should probably take her own advice.

He took out his phone.

'Wh-what are you doing?'

'Ringing the police.'

Oh, that wasn't good.

Sybella didn't think, she just made a snatch for his phone. It wasn't the cleverest thing she could have done, but once the area's constabulary were involved this would be around the village in a flash. Her parents-in-law already thought she wasn't handling her life to their satisfaction. It would be another reason why she and Fleur should move in with them.

He held the phone just out of her reach, which was easy for him, given he appeared to be a god stepped down from Asgard. Sybella wouldn't have been surprised if he'd grabbed a stake of lightning while he was at it. Only he was looking down at her as if she were a puppy with muddy paws that had suddenly decided to jump on him.

It was beyond frustrating.

'Please,' she tried again, 'this is just a misunderstanding.'

'*Nyet*, this is trespass. I want you off my property.'

Sybella shook her head in disbelief. 'Are you going to let me explain?'

'*Nyet*.'

She stepped up to him and laid her hand on his forearm. 'Please, you have to listen. I'm not a trespasser.'

He frowned.

'I've never trespassed in my life. Not knowingly.'

Which was when the committee members of the Heritage Trust appeared out of the side entrance of Edbury Hall, humming like a hive of wasps.

Sybella's heart began to beat so fast she seriously thought she might pass out.

'Who in the hell are they?' he demanded, because clearly nothing was getting past this guy.

'The Heritage Trust committee,' she croaked. This was a disaster! She had to go and warn them.

Turning quickly, she didn't notice the bag at her feet until her boot caught on it and Sybella found herself for the second time tonight arms extended, launched head first for the snow.

Strong hands caught her around the waist and literally lifted her, this time bringing her into contact with his big, hard body. Instinctively she wrapped her arms around his neck. It was the wrong move. Sensation zipped through her body like an electrical charge and it dipped right between her legs.

Sybella panicked and tried to pull away but he had her held tight.

'Stop wriggling,' he ordered gruffly and she stopped. Mainly because her face was dangerously close to his and a part of her was finding the physical contact thrilling.

'Can you—just—look, stop holding me!' She was mumbling this into his bare neck, because apparently he thought hugging her to him was a good idea.

It wasn't. Even with the layers of fabric between them she'd been a man-free zone for so long it was like landing on planet Mars and discovering there wasn't enough gravity to hold you down. Worse, he smelt awfully good, manly in a way she had forgotten, and, combined with his warm solidity, she was beginning to enjoy all the contact.

Not interested in sex? She'd clearly sent a message out into the universe and the sneaky gods had sent down one of their own to make a liar of her.

'Please,' she begged, turning her face to meet his eyes, which was a mistake because he was looking back at her and they were dangerously close.

She could see how thick his golden eyelashes were, and his eyes had seemingly soaked up the colours around them like the Northern Lights she'd seen on a documentary about the Arctic. She could have sworn a moment ago they were icy grey.

Her panicked breath caught and everything telescoped down to his amazing eyes before his gaze swooped to her mouth. He looked as if he was going to kiss her or was that just her idea?

Panic renewed, Sybella began to thrash about in earnest. 'Please let me go before this all gets out of hand!'

On the contrary, Nik was confident he had it all in hand.

He would deal with the small tide of humanity edging towards them, and then he would find out why there appeared to be no security at all in operation at his grandfather's home.

But first he needed to deal with what he had in his arms, the problem being he wasn't sure what that was. He'd turned his head to find something other than what he'd first imagined. She had a vivid face, eyes that seemed to be searching his and the kind of sensuous full mouth that gave men creative thoughts. She also smelt of flowers, which was distracting him. He set her down in the snow.

'Do not move,' he told her.

He went around to the cab of the SUV and turned on the headlights to high beam, capturing the dozen rugged-up intruders like a spotlight on a stage.

'I'm Nikolai Aleksandrovich Voronov,' he said in a deep voice that didn't need to be raised. On its own it carried across the front façade of the house and possibly beyond. 'If you're not off the estate in the next two minutes, I'll have you all arrested for trespass.'

He didn't wait to see what they would do. He knew what they would do. Scatter and run.

Nik hoisted his bag over his shoulder and gave his attention to the unhappy girl, standing there encased in what looked like cladding. In the dark she no longer looked like the sensual siren he'd imagined a moment ago and was back to being the abominable snowman.

'You can go with your friends,' he said with a curt nod, before turning his back on her.

Sleet was falling more heavily as he approached the house.

He used the side entrance lit by lamp posts that glowed through the snowy gloom like something out of *The Lion, The Witch and The Wardrobe*, a book his Anglophile grandfather had given to him when he was a boy. No wonder the old man loved the place. Nik saw only an investment and right now a heavy oak door he pushed open with his shoulder.

He was aware he'd been followed, alerted by his companion's crunching footsteps over the stones and her hitching breath, because clearly the woman was out of shape with all that extra weight she was carrying.

He waited for Rapunzel because he wasn't in the habit of closing doors in women's faces. Another glance reinforced what he already knew. She was tall, abetted by a pair of what looked like hiking boots, and the parka and trousers gave her a square look not identifiable as female in the dark.

'What do you want?'

She had planted herself just inside the threshold.

'To explain.'

'I'm not interested.'

She stepped towards him, clearly reluctant, the light falling full on her.

She was wearing the ski mask now as a beanie, most of her astonishing hair caught up inside it. She had full cheeks pink from the cold and her hazel eyes he'd already established were bright, but it was her lush pink mouth that drew the eye.

'Actually, about that…you probably do want to talk to me.'

Nik had it on the tip of his tongue to tell her while she looked like a Christmas angel he wouldn't be changing his mind.

Instead he gave her a moment to clarify.

'I work here.'

She was staff? Why in hell hadn't she said so?

'I'm Sybella,' she said. 'Sybella Parminter.'

Nik took a moment to reconcile the girl standing in front of him with the woman with the wellington boots and the face like a shovel. He'd underestimated his grandfather. The old man had rigged a honey trap.

Nik crossed the floor to her in a few strides and, before she could react, reached behind her head and yanked off the ski mask.

Her hair tumbled out.

'What are you doing?' she demanded, lifting her bemittened hands to her head in a protective gesture, as if he might start pulling at her hair again.

It was exactly as it had looked in the snow, heavy and flaxen blonde almost all the way down to her waist. The electric light made it shimmer, or maybe he was just tired and even ordinary women were beginning to look like goddesses.

That fast a picture took shape of a golden angel ministering to his grandfather and putting ideas in his head about English heritage and great-grandchildren while she eyed the title deeds to the house.

'You can't just manhandle me,' she said, pushing back her hair self-consciously and eyeing him as if he were a wolf about to leap at her. He also saw the feminine awareness kindling in her eyes and knew exactly how he was going to handle this.

'Call me Nik.'

'Nik,' she said warily, taking a big step back. 'Well, I would like the opportunity to explain. If I could come back tomorrow?'

'I think you will stay where you are.'

'But you just told me to go.'

'Glad you're keeping up.'

She blinked.

'What were you doing outside?'

Sybella didn't know whether to run for her life or stand her ground. His pulling and pushing, not to mention the way he'd looked at her hair as if it were some kind of man snare, had left her unnerved. But she had people relying on her. She couldn't let them down.

'The Heritage Trust meet here on Thursday nights. I'm secretary. Assistant secretary.' She took a breath. Honesty was the best policy. 'I'm the only one who can do short-hand. We don't use a recording device.'

'You don't run it?'

'Well, no.'

He was shrugging out of his coat, looking around the entrance hall as if expecting minions to appear and help him. 'So you don't run it, you're the secretary. How long has this been going on?' he asked.

'A little under a year. Mr Voronov was kind enough—'

'For you to take advantage.'

'No, that's not—'

Sybella promptly lost her train of thought as the tailored wool slid down his arms and she discovered what had felt so solid outside when she'd been holding onto him. An expensive-looking charcoal sweater clung to broad shoulders and a long, hard, lean waist, apparently packed with bricks. Narrow muscled hips and long powerful legs filled out his dark jeans. By the time she reached his big, got-to-be-size-fifteen hand-tooled boots the tour had effectively rendered Sybella slightly dazzled and a whole lot mute.

She realised she'd just checked him out.

It was either her silence or the raptness of her regard that had him look up from shaking out his coat and give her that once-over thing men did, the subtle up and down assessment as to whether or not he'd consider sleeping with her…and Sybella had the humiliating thought he'd caught her staring and assumed she was doing the same thing.

Which she was. Unintentionally. Not because she was considering sleeping with him. Goodness, no. She hadn't *meant* to ogle him. It had just happened. But he didn't know that.

What made it worse was the Climb and Ski gear had currently turned her perfectly nice woman's body into a flotation device and the likelihood of him finding anything attractive about her was zilch.

'Care to tell me what you were really doing jumping out at me in the dark?' His eyes held a new awareness now that she'd pretty much flagged she found him attractive.

Sybella could feel her cheeks hot as coals. He made her feel like a teenage girl with a boy she liked. It was ridiculous at her advanced age of twenty-eight.

'I didn't jump out at you. You threw luggage at me!' He had moved across to the open boot-room door to hang up his coat. Sybella followed him, a tiny tug boat to his tanker.

'I expected to be greeted by staff,' he said.

She guessed that put her in her place. Sybella surreptitiously admired his rear, which like the rest of him appeared to be pure muscle, which was when he just tossed the grenade in.

'I also thought you were a man.'

And there went what was left of her self-image tonight.

'Wh-what?' she bleated, like a stupid lamb for slaughter.

'I mean, obviously you're not,' he said, frowning at her as if he'd just noticed her stricken expression and was assessing what it meant.

'No,' she choked, 'not a man. Thanks.'

'It was dark and you're wearing unisex clothing.' He was hanging up his coat, drawing attention to the flex of muscles along his back.

'This isn't unisex.' Sybella looked down at her considerable padded bulk. 'It's oyster-pink.'

His expression told her he didn't make the connection.

'Pink is traditionally a female colour,' she spelt out.

He continued to look doubtful.

She huffed out a breath. 'Look, this parka was clearly marked "Women Size L" on the rack,' she insisted. Then stopped.

Had she just informed him she was size large?

Yes—yes, she had.

'It was dark,' he repeated, and the frown was back.

He closed the door behind him, crowding her back out into the corridor.

When she picked up her bruised and bloodied self-esteem from the floor, Sybella would remind herself she was tall, wearing layers and a ski mask, and he was right—it was dark. Her throat felt tight, because it wasn't *that* dark.

Sybella only felt worse when he took the main stairs with an effortless stride that left her labouring as best she could in his wake, because by now she was not only wet through, the all-weather gear was making it difficult to move freely.

It begged the question how people climbed mountains in these things when she was finding a staircase hard going.

She was a little out of breath at the top.

'You need to get a bit more exercise,' he said, stopping to look down at her. 'You're out of shape.'

Really? That was what he had to say to her? The only time she ever got to sit down was on a quiet afternoon at the records office where she worked.

'Shouldn't you be on your way up to see your grandfather?' she said instead, no longer at all keen to explain anything to him. She just wanted to go home. Preferably to a hot bath where she could enjoy a little cry.

'He'll keep.'

He'll keep? What sort of grandson was he? Well, she knew the answer to that. The absent kind. She scowled at his back. If he hadn't been absent she wouldn't be in this fix.

Sybella followed him down the Long Gallery. She regularly conducted tours of this room, pointing out the features, recounting the history of the house. She suspected Mr I-thought-you-were-a-man wouldn't be very happy if he knew.

There were six Jacobean chairs piled up in the middle of the room, awaiting a home.

'What in the hell?' he said, circling them.

She opted for a cheerful, 'Don't you love these? Your

grandfather had them brought down from storage in the attics. We haven't worked out where to put them.'

'We?' He rounded on her. 'You're interested in the contents of the house?'

As if she were some kind of criminal. Sybella found herself backing up a bit. 'No, I'm interested in the past.'

'Why?'

A little flustered by the way he was looking at her, all suspicious and hard-eyed but making her feel very much a woman despite what he'd said, she found herself struggling for an answer. 'I don't know. I just am.'

He looked unimpressed.

She had to do better. She rummaged around for something he'd believe. 'If you grew up like I did in a very modern house in a relentlessly upmarket housing estate you'd see the beauty in old things too.'

He looked skeptical.

'It was the most soulless place on this green earth. I knew from an early age there had to be something better. More meaningful.'

Sybella took a breath, realising she'd told him a little more than she had meant to.

'Why does furniture have more meaning if it's old?'

'Because old things have stories attached to them, and the furniture that's survived tends to have been made by craftsmen and women. Artists.'

'You're a romantic,' he said, again as if this were a crime.

'No, I'm practical.' She'd had to be. 'Although I guess as a child I read books about other children who lived in old houses and fantasised that might be me one day.'

'Is that so?'

Nik was tempted to ask her if she could see herself in this house.

'It's not unusual,' she said defensively. 'Lots of children have thoughts like that, and I had a good reason to.'

Nik suspected he was about to hear a sob story. He was also aware if he gave her enough rope she'd probably happily hang herself. She was nervous around him and it was making her talk.

'I'm more curious about your interest in this house,' he growled.

'No, you asked me why I was interested in the past.'

He added pedantic to overweight and possibly a con-artist.

'Old houses, miserable childhood, check.'

'I didn't say I had a miserable childhood.' She looked affronted. 'I said the house was soulless,' she said firmly. 'We were the only people who had ever lived there. Which was ironic.'

'I'll bite—why?'

She tried to fold her arms, which was rendered difficult by the bulk of her clothing. 'Because the woman who raised me was obsessed with genealogy. Her genealogy, not mine, as it turned out.'

'You were adopted?'

She nodded, for the first time looking less communicative. Her pretty face was closed up like a fist.

He'd been fifteen when he was told his father was not his father, and Nik had always looked at his life in terms of *before* and *after*.

'When did you find out?'

She looked up at him as if gauging whether to tell him. 'I was twelve. It was when my parents separated.'

'Must have been difficult.'

'Yes,' she said. 'It was more difficult when they handed me back.'

'They handed you back?'

She was radiating tension now. 'Dumped me in a very nice boarding school and left me there for six years.'

He almost laughed. *That* was her complaint?

Spoilt upper-class girl still bemoaning her school years at what—going by her elocution—was an upmarket school. He wondered what else she had to complain about. And here he was, actually feeling sorry for her.

She was good, he had to give her that.

'Have you ever considered they were giving you a good education?'

'They gave me a very good education,' she said tonelessly, looking down at her clasped hands. She probably understood her bid for sympathy was going nowhere. 'But I saw them very rarely in the term breaks and now not at all. It was as good as handing me back.'

Sybella was pleased with her command of herself and that she could talk about her adoptive parents in a forthright way. He'd asked the questions; she'd merely answered them. No external emotion needed.

Only for all her firmness on the subject she could feel the cold running like a tap inside her and she would have trouble turning it off tonight.

'That is a sad little story,' he said, something in his tone making her think he didn't quite believe her.

She suddenly felt self-conscious and slightly annoyed. 'I guess it is. I don't know why I told you all that. I'm sure it's not at all interesting to a man like yourself.'

'You'd be surprised what interests me.'

Sybella discovered she didn't have anything smart to say in answer to that. But she couldn't help running her gaze over his broad shoulders, remembering how strong and sure he'd felt holding her.

His eyes caught hers and something flared between them. 'And what exactly interests you, Miss Parminter?'

Sybella knew what interested her, and it wasn't going to happen.

She could feel her face filling up with heat.

'It's Mrs,' she stated baldly in a desperate attempt to deflect whatever he might say next. 'Mrs Parminter.'

'You're married?'

There had been a current of awareness zipping between them from the time she'd been grappling with him in the snow, only Sybella didn't know that until this very second as it was sucked back to nothingness and what was left was a tense, awkward silence.

Sybella didn't know what to say.

But he did.

'Does your husband know you're out at night running around with other men?'

CHAPTER FOUR

WITH TOO MANY bad memories still beating around in her head something snapped inside Sybella, enough to have her hand arcing through the air.

Fortunately his reflexes were quicker than hers and he gripped her wrist, holding her immobile.

There was a fraught silence in which all she could hear was her pulse drumming in her ears. Then he said quietly, 'That was out of line,' releasing her arm so that Sybella could slowly lower it to her side.

'It's none of my business,' he added. Which was when she realised he wasn't talking about her trying to hit him. He was apologising for what he'd said.

The fight went out of Sybella, and with it flooded in the knowledge she'd almost hit another person.

Last year Fleur had pushed over a little boy in her social group and Sybella had sat down and had the talk with her. Physically hurting someone was wrong. Whatever the provocation, she must use her words, not her fists. And here she was, mother of the year, trying to slug a perfect stranger!

She'd had provocation all right, but that wasn't an excuse.

She needed to apologise to him but Sybella found herself struggling because he'd implied something, and he hadn't taken that back. Which was very different from saying it was *none of his business*.

'Six years ago my husband kissed me and climbed into his van and drove it out to the Pentwistle Farm,' she said in a low voice, 'and on the road between the farm and the turn-off he was struck by another car coming over the rise.'

Nik was looking at her with an expression she hadn't seen before in this man.

As if he were taking her seriously.

'So no, Mr Voronov, my husband has no idea what I'm doing nowadays—but I do. I wish I hadn't tried to hit you. I can't take that back. But you don't get to say things like that to me. I don't deserve your contempt, or do you just have a problem with women in general? I suspect you do.'

Sybella had no idea where all those words had come from or her ability to say them or even if they were true. But nothing had just 'happened' here tonight. It had been building since he'd held her in his arms outside in the snow and all the sensuality latent in her body had woken up.

She resented it, and she resented him. But none of that was his fault.

'I suspect I have a problem with you, Mrs Parminter,' he said slowly. 'But I am sorry for what I said.'

'You should be.' She held his gaze. She could see her words had affected him and she could also see some grudging respect in his eyes and that gave her the grace to say, 'I'm sorry too.'

She forced the apology out, because as wrong as her actions were she couldn't yet let go of them, or the feelings that had provoked them. None of this had made her feel better; she felt worse. She wrapped arms around her waist as best she could in her ridiculous parka.

He was looking at her as if she deserved some compassion. He was wrong. She deserved a good talking-to for all the mistakes she'd made in dealing with this house.

'You're cold,' he said. 'You need to take off your wet things.'

'I don't—'

'You can dry them in front of the fire, or I can have them laundered.'

'Please don't bother.' She passed a hand over her face.

'I'm going to take them back to Climb and Ski tomorrow for a full refund.'

'Are you all right?'

She blinked, taking her hand away from her face to find him watching her as if she might keel over. 'I guess so.'

Which was when her eyes filled with tears. *Oh, blast.*

Tired, wet, in some serious trouble over her activities in this house, and yet troublingly aware of Nik Voronov as a man and her own deficiencies in that area, Sybella wanted nothing more than to wriggle out of her wet things and cast herself down in front of the fire and sleep for a hundred years.

But she didn't get the fairy-tale option. She should be practising a better apology.

There was a rattle and clatter as Gordon, who ran the household, entered from a side door, wheeling the drinks trolley.

Saved by the man with the alcohol!

A long-time bachelor, Gordon was her ally in the house, having worked here for almost thirty years under the previous owner. He gave her a guarded look of surprise but didn't say anything. He was too good at his job.

Her host meanwhile had signalled to Gordon he could deal with the drinks.

Sybella wondered if she could just slip out with the trolley. But the fire lured her and she turned away to deal with her wet things, surreptitiously sniffing and wiping at her eyes with her wrist. She stripped off her parka and then her cords, feeling self-conscious in her tights but not exposed. They were of a durable denier and thick enough to act as leggings. Frankly, it was a relief to be able to move her body freely again.

She laid out her jeans before the fire and had just straightened up when a towel dropped over her head.

She gave a start but with a gruff, 'Hold still,' her host began to vigorously but not roughly rub dry her damp hair.

After an initial protest of, 'I can do this,' she gave in, because really he was impossible to argue with.

But this was her role. For five years she'd been the care-giver. It was disconcerting to find herself the one being cared for. And as his strokes became more rhythmic Sybella found herself going quiescent, some of the tension of the crazy evening leaving her.

It had been so long since her needs were seen to by someone else. She'd forgotten it could be like this. Even when Simon had been alive he'd been so busy with his new veterinary practice in the few months they were married they had seemed only to bump into each other at night in bed, and Sybella could feel her skin suffusing with heat because another man's hands were on her, if only drying her hair. But when she looked up and clashed with his grey eyes she was shocked into feelings so raw and insistent she barely recognised them as the gentle, awkward finding their way she'd had with Simon...

'That's enough,' she said, her voice a little rough with the sudden upsurge of feeling beating around in her.

He paused but then continued to dry her even more vigorously.

'If you collapse from pneumonia in a few days' time—' he said gruffly.

'You don't want it on your conscience?'

'I don't want a lawsuit.'

Sybella snorted, she couldn't help it, and she felt rather than saw him smile.

'I'm not a lawyer,' she said, 'and I don't have the money for a lawyer.'

'What do you do,' he asked, removing the towel so that her head came back and she could see him, 'besides haunt this house?'

She didn't miss a beat. 'I could give you a list?'

A slow grudging smile curled up his mouth, taking Sybella's entire attention with it. 'Why don't you do that?'

As if he had all the time in the world to listen to her life story. As if like before she'd spill her guts.

Instead she asked, 'Why don't you visit your grandfather more often?' It was the one thing that really bothered her, and it was more important than anything to do with the open house and how much trouble she would be in.

He reached out and gently smoothed the drying ringlets back from her face.

'I would have visited earlier,' he said, 'if I'd had any idea something so beautiful was here.'

Then his gaze dropped to her mouth.

She relived that moment in the snow and realised it hadn't been her imagination. There was a very strong attraction between them.

Only she didn't do things like this.

Given the last man to kiss her existed now only in her memory of him.

She wasn't even sure what she would do if he...

His mouth covered hers. He gave her no opportunity to back out, or overthink it, he just made it happen. One hand sliding around the back of her head to cradle her, the other at the small of her back. His hand was so broad he could span her waist from behind.

In a flurry of sense impressions, Sybella had never felt so delicate, so utterly aware she was a feeling, sensate woman and, as exciting and dangerous as this was, she felt completely safe in his arms.

Where he had been so rough with her out in the snow he was now showing due care and acknowledgement of her as a female, which put to bed his remark about mistaking her for a man and engendered a fluttery feeling inside her. It bloomed high in her chest and a swirling warmth gathered down below.

He brought her in close to his body and she felt the full hard, muscular strength of him and it was enough.

She gave way, her mouth softening under his, the entire lost art of kissing returning to her with some subtle but much appreciated changes.

His tongue touched, grazed, tasted, seduced and the feel of him was so completely male and so overwhelming in the certainty of his approach Sybella took what he gave her instinctively and with an utter disregard to where this might be leading.

Until all her doubts came rushing back in and she ducked her head.

'What's wrong?' he asked gruffly.

Apart from he was a stranger, and they didn't know one another, and she suspected given her activities in his house only trouble could come from this?

'I don't know.' She did know—she was feeling a bit too much and it had been so long and she no longer had any certainty in her ability to meet him as a sexually confident woman. But had she ever?

She wasn't ready for this.

Meg would say whatever sense of herself as a desirable woman had been shoved into the back of her wardrobe in a box along with her preserved wedding bouquet and all the plans she and Simon had made for the future. But it had happened before that. It had happened when Simon had briefly dated another girl and slept with her.

It was a little disconcerting to say the least to discover, gazing up at this intense, beautiful man, she had no idea where to go from here with him. But she did know one thing. She had to let him know what was going on in his house.

'I have to tell you something,' she blurted out. 'Edbury Hall is open to the public on weekends.'

Nik didn't immediately let her go. His hand was still curled around her sweet waist gloved in soft cashmere wool that made the most of her glorious curves above and below.

He could pinpoint the moment he'd stopped thinking clearly. It was when he'd seen her bending down by the fire, the most female-looking woman. She was the proverbial hourglass, and if there was a little more sand than was standard in that glass his libido didn't make that distinction. She had ample breasts and long, shapely legs, deliciously plump around her thighs and bottom, and in his arms she'd felt like both comfort and sin.

Which explained why his brain took a little longer to catch up, because his body was happy where it was, Sybella's curves giving him a full body press.

'Why is the house open to the public?' He forced himself to set her back. 'On whose authorisation?'

'Mr Voronov senior's, and—and yours.' Sybella's voice gave out, so the 'yours' wasn't much more than a whisper.

'Mine?' he growled, any trace of the man who had begun to kiss her and rouse such passionate feelings in her evaporating like the last patch of sunshine on a cold winter's day.

'You were sent the paperwork. I didn't just go ahead only on your grandfather's say-so,' she protested.

'I received no paperwork.'

No. She gnawed on the inside of her lip. Now she would have to explain about the letters. But she didn't want to be responsible for a further breach between grandfather and grandson. Family was important.

No one understood that better than someone who for a long time didn't have any.

No, it would be better if his grandfather confessed.

And what if Nik Voronov decided to blame her anyway?

Blood was blood, and old Mr Voronov might easily side with his grandson.

Sybella knew she had nobody to blame but herself and for a spinning moment she just started babbling. 'I don't see who has been hurt by any of this. Mr Voronov is a lonely man and he enjoys having people into the house…'

'And you have taken advantage of that.'

'No!' Sybella closed her eyes and took a breath. Arguing with him wasn't going to accomplish anything. 'I understand you don't know me,' she said, keeping her voice as steady as she could, given the escalating tension, 'and you say you're worried about your grandfather—'

'I am worried about him.'

'Well, I don't see any evidence of that given you're never here!'

Oh, she should have kept that to herself. And now he was looking down at her without a shred of give in him.

'I suspect you've taken my grandfather for a ride, and, if I find out that's the case, you really don't want me for an enemy Mrs Parminter.'

It was difficult not to take a step back.

She swallowed hard. 'Do you go through life mistrusting people?'

'When it comes to my family I don't allow anything past the keeper.'

Those words took the indignant air out of her because she guarded her little family too. His grandfather had become of late an honorary member of that family and for a moment she wondered if *she'd* got it wrong. Nik Voronov might genuinely care about his grandfather. If the shoe were on the other foot she would be suspicious too.

She tried again. 'Honestly, Nik, it's not what you think.'

'I think we can probably go back to Mr Voronov.'

He was making her feel as if she'd done something wrong.

Which was when she noticed he was getting out his phone.

'Are you calling the police again?' She tried not to sound despairing because, really, what were they going to arrest her on? Impersonating a married lady? Kissing a man she'd just met?

'I'm arranging a car for you. I take it you live in the village?'

It was no more than a ten-minute walk if she took the lane, but Sybella didn't intend to argue with him about the lift.

'If this is your organisation's way of drumming up support you can let them know that honey traps went out in the nineteen seventies.'

Honey trap?

He turned away and spoke rapidly into his phone in Russian.

Sybella wondered if being shaken about like a child's toy earlier had affected her hearing. It had certainly loosened some of her native intelligence.

What did he think, she was Mata Hari kissing men for state secrets?

Oh, boy, she definitely needed to get out of here.

Cursing her own stupidity, she pulled on her damp jeans and then bent down to reattach her boots. Everything was cold and unpleasant and would chafe but there was no helping that.

'I want you back here nice and early, let's say eight o'clock for breakfast,' he said from behind her. 'You have some explaining to do, and it will be in the presence of my grandfather.'

Sybella became aware he was probably getting a really good look at her wide womanly behind at this moment.

But everything was such a shambles—what was one more humiliation?

'Eight o'clock is too early.'

'Tough. Get an alarm clock.'

She straightened up. 'For your information I'll be awake at six, but I have a great deal to organise myself. You're not the only busy person in the world, Mr Voronov.'

He looked unimpressed.

'I am running a billion-dollar business, Mrs Parminter. What's your excuse?'

A five-year-old girl, Sybella thought, eyeing him narrowly, but he looked like one of those unreconstructed dinosaurs who thought raising children happened by magic. Besides, she was not bringing her daughter into this hostile conversation.

'The fact is I'm out of here tomorrow,' he informed her. 'Let's call this your window of opportunity.'

'To do what?'

'To convince me not to involve my lawyers.'

All the fight went out of Sybella. She couldn't quite believe this was happening. But she told herself surely old Mr Voronov would clear the air tomorrow.

'Fine. I'll be here.'

To her surprise he took his wool coat and handed it to her with a less antagonistic, 'You'll need this.'

Sybella looked at her Climb and Ski jacket she'd been unable to bring herself to put back on and self-consciously drew his coat around her shoulders.

The gesture reminded her of how kind he'd been drying her hair, how he'd made her feel cared for if only for a brief time. It was enough to make her want to cry, and she hated crying. It didn't change anything.

She turned away from him, his scent surrounding her inside the coat.

She spotted the bottle of brandy and on a whim picked

it up. After the events of this evening she needed it more than he did.

He didn't say anything and when she went downstairs to climb into the waiting car she was holding it to her like a safety blanket.

Stupid really, when she didn't drink. Stupid being in this car, when it would take only ten minutes or five minutes if she'd legged it. She brought her fingertips to her mouth. It still felt a little swollen and sensitive from all the attention. Stupid, probably, to have kissed him.

CHAPTER FIVE

'MUMMY, THERE'S A GIANT standing in our garden. What do you think about that?'

Given yesterday it had been an elephant under the stairs, Sybella didn't rush to call the fire brigade or police station or even Jack the giant killer.

When she did put away the bath towels she was folding and came into her bedroom, she found her five-year-old daughter was kneeling at the dormer window in her pyjamas, her big violet-blue eyes full of innocent curiosity for a world that produced fairy-tale characters in human guise.

Joining Fleur at the glass, she obligingly looked out. Her pulse hit a thousand and she stepped back and said a silent prayer. Then she leaned forward again to get a better look.

She became aware of Fleur watching her, waiting for a cue as to how to respond to this stranger at their door. Sybella shook off her astonishment.

'That's not a giant, darling, that's a Viking god.'

He was facing their door and in a minute he'd work out the old-fashioned bell-pull was indeed the bell—but it was broken.

Then he'd probably pound on the door until he broke it down.

'Mummy will go down and speak to him. Why don't you stay here with Dodge? You know how nervous he gets around boys.'

'Because they're noisy.' Fleur picked up her toy bricks and returned to fitting pieces together. Sybella wasn't fooled. Her daughter would wait until the coast was clear and make her way to the top of the stairs and peer down through the bannisters.

Sybella wouldn't have minded that option herself. Instead she took the stairs by twos, then stopped in front of the hall mirror and checked her face was clean. Clean but her eyes were shadowed with lack of sleep.

She'd been on the Internet late last night checking up on Nik Voronov and how much damage he could possibly do her. Given he was on the *Forbes* list, probably a lot.

At least she was wearing her work clothes: a white silk blouse, a knee-length caramel-coloured suede skirt and boots. Pretty respectable. She ran a hand through her yet-to-be-braided hair and went to open the door.

Then hesitated and looked at herself in the glass again, this time undoing her top two buttons.

There, just a hint of cleavage. It had nothing to do with making herself more attractive for the man who had called her a honey trap last night. It was about her own self-confidence as a woman.

She opened the door, and her self-confidence did a wobble and promptly fell over.

He was wearing a tailored suit and tie. He might as well have been wearing a surcoat and carrying a broadsword. She knew he'd come to take prisoners.

His eyes flared over her as if he were dropping a net and Sybella instinctively dug her heels into her shoes to keep herself from being dragged in towards him.

And just like last night in the snow it was his mouth she was drawn to. The wide lower lip, the slight curve at the ends that could go either way, like Nero's thumb, up or down, and decide your fate. She'd been kissed by that mouth last night and it had definitely been going her way for a little bit. But in the end it had all been a ruse to make her look as foolish as possible.

'Enjoy the brandy?'

The brandy? She hadn't known what to do with the

bottle when she'd got home so she'd stashed it in the linen closet.

It had occurred to her that Catherine, her mother-in-law, was regularly in and out of that cupboard when she babysat Fleur.

Sybella was forever coming home to freshly changed sheets, which she appreciated even as it drove her crazy.

Hiding spirits behind the bathroom towels, Sybella, dear?

A little devil she didn't know was in her made her say, 'Yes, thank you, I drank the lot.'

'Careful,' he said, his deep voice wiping away any comparisons with her mother-in-law, 'excessive drinking is a slippery slope to all kinds of illness in later life.'

'I'll keep that in mind.'

What did he want? Why was he looking at her in that way, his eyes trained on her, cool and watchful and somehow taking her clothes off?

'So,' she said, swallowing. 'How can I help you today?'

Nik eyed the two undone buttons.

'It's nine o'clock.'

'I told you my mornings were busy.' She made a gesture with her hand, wriggling her fingers. 'Serene on the surface, duck legs churning underneath.'

Nik's attention had drifted to her hair because it seemed to have grown more abundant overnight like some Victorian-era maiden. He suddenly found himself right back where he was last night. Wanting her.

He cleared his throat. 'My grandfather tells me you take tours of the house.'

She stood a little straighter. 'The third Thursday of every month, we have school groups in. Only in the west wing.'

'You bring people into my house?'

'I don't think your grandfather considers the house

yours,' she said, her fan of lashes flickering nervously. 'Really the house belongs to everyone in Edbury in a manner of speaking. There has been a manor house on this spot since the time of the Normans—'

'Fascinating.'

'It is fascinating!' She firmed her mouth. 'Your grandfather understands we're only caretakers of a place like this. That's why he agreed to open up the estate again to the public.'

Nik tried not to notice how her blouse hugged her breasts or her skirt flared over those rounded hips. 'I am more interested in discovering exactly why my property is being treated like a theme park.'

Sybella's heart sank. If this was his attitude there was no win for her here.

Only she noticed his gaze was roaming a little too far south of her face again and she could feel her body responding, the warmth rising up into her cheeks, the backs of her knees tingling.

'I'm not a theme park either,' she said flatly.

To her surprise a streak of colour rose over his high, flat cheekbones.

'And no one is treating Edbury Hall that way,' she hastened on, wanting to put the sexual awareness behind them where it belonged. 'It's more of an educational facility.'

He folded his arms. 'Who is paying your salary?'

'No one. Everyone volunteers.'

'Right.'

'No one's ever been paid at Edbury. All takings are funnelled back into other projects in the area.'

His gaze zeroed in on her. 'You're not an employee?'

She shook her head.

'Good, that makes this less ambiguous.'

'What do you mean "ambiguous"? What's ambiguous?' Sybella didn't like the sound of that.

He looked up at the lintel above her head and over the local stone that walled her house.

'You're also my tenant,' he spelt out, cool gaze dropping to hers once more. 'The lease on the Hall includes these weavers' cottages.'

'Yes,' she said feeling hunted, 'and I've never missed a rental payment.'

'Nobody said you had. But just as a hypothetical example, how would you like it if I turned this row into a tourist attraction on the weekends?'

'They are a tourist attraction.'

'Prostit?'

'People come from all over the world to photograph our cottages. Several film crews have been on site in this street in the past four years.' She folded her arms across her chest. 'I'm beginning to think you know nothing of Edbury at all.'

'You'd be right. I own the Hall for tax purposes.'

'I'm sorry?'

'I'm required to own a certain amount of property in the UK for tax reasons.'

She stared at him as if he'd announced he'd stolen the Crown Jewels and was currently storing them in the Kremlin.

'You must be joking? You've caused all this upset in the village because you want to cheat on your tax?' Her voice had risen exponentially.

Nik shifted on his size fifteens. 'I do not engage in illegal activities, Mrs Parminter, and I would be careful about what you say to me.'

She looked taken aback and retreated a little into the safety of her doorway.

Nik expelled a deep breath. He did not bully women, but every conversation with this girl turned into a confrontation.

'I'm not interested in your financial dealings, Mr Voronov,' she said, looking persecuted, 'any more than I enjoy being doorstepped at nine o'clock in the morning. Say what you've got to say and go.'

He looked her up and down, which she clearly didn't like.

'I've said it.'

'Good.'

She took another step back into her house and began to close her door. But he hadn't finished with her yet.

'Anything more you'd care to tell me before the lawyers get involved?'

She halted and then stuck her head out again. 'What do you mean "lawyers"?'

'I seem to have an echo,' he observed.

She pinned her lips together and those hazel eyes fixed pensively on him as she stepped reluctantly outside again.

'I—I hardly think lawyers are necessary.'

'Fortunately that decision is mine.'

Awful man. Why was he so set on blaming her for everything? And why was she still finding it difficult not to drink in every last masculine inch of him?

Sybella tried to find something reasonable to say but what popped out was, 'Why are you down here bothering people?'

He leaned in a little closer.

'I told you,' he said in that fathom-deep voice. 'I am visiting my grandfather.'

Sybella could have told him right now it didn't feel that way. After the events of last night it felt as if he were visiting her! For purposes that felt entirely too hormonal on her behalf.

'Well, perhaps if you'd bothered to turn up before now you'd know what was going on here,' she threw back at him a little desperately, 'instead of stomping around like a big bully and making everyone go through lawyers.'

'Given I'm based in St Petersburg, turning up isn't that simple.'

'Is that where you live?' The question just slipped out, openly curious, and Sybella knew she'd given herself away. Her stupid interest in him.

She could feel the heat rushing into her face.

'Da,' he said, and there was a silence during which Sybella remembered how much she'd told him about her life last night. The intimacy that had created.

'Well, maybe it isn't so easy for you to get down here regularly,' she admitted reluctantly, 'but your grandfather needs family around him at this time of his life.'

His eyes iced over. 'My grandfather is well taken care of.'

'Is he? Do you know he doesn't like his nurse? He doesn't trust her.'

Nik frowned. 'He hasn't said anything to me.'

'Perhaps if you visited once in a while you could talk to the people around him who matter, not the people you're employing, and you might have a better idea of what's really going on instead of making up these stupid stories and—and picking on me!'

'And you're one of the people who matter?' he asked.

'I don't matter, but I am here. I do see what goes on.'

Nik didn't like the picture she painted, that his grandfather was unhappy, that in some way he was failing.

Only her hands had migrated to her hips again, and he was finding it difficult not to be distracted by the way her chest lifted every time she made her point and the button holding back the mystery of her cleavage strained.

'Here's what I think, Mrs Parminter. You've been using my grandfather's kindness to benefit yourself.'

'Yes, you would think that.'

Sybella glared back at him.

The truth was so much more simple and delightful than anything this man could make up in his suspicious mind.

His grandfather had forged one of those charming intergenerational friendships with her small daughter.

Sybella had watched a lonely and reserved man come to life in the company of her forthright, imaginative Fleur, and the sight of Mr Voronov's white head bent over a book with Fleur's small dark one as they read together made every Thursday afternoon a treasure.

Fleur didn't come easily to reading. She was a child who wanted to be out of doors, climbing trees, chasing cows and getting muddy. All the things possible because they lived in the country. She was, in short, very much like her late father.

Simon had always struggled with reading comprehension and he wouldn't want his daughter to go through that.

His own father shared the same difficulty.

Mr Voronov was a godsend.

Furthering her career had been the last thing on her mind.

But she wasn't telling this man any of that.

She'd told him too much in her stupid confessional last night.

It was her business. It wasn't any of his.

'Frankly, I don't care what you happen to think. I am going to continue to visit your grandfather and there's nothing you can do about it!'

Sybella's soaring moment of satisfaction was short-lived.

'Mrs Parminter, let me tell you how it's going to be.' His voice had dropped to a calm dead certainty. 'Your visits to the house are over. You are to stay away or there will be consequences. Are we clear?'

'What consequences?'

'Legal consequences.'

The colour had gone; not a scrap of it remained in her face.

Nik waited to feel satisfied by that. He didn't. But he damn well wasn't taking ultimatums from this woman. Dealing with this had already taken up too much of his valuable time.

'Listen, I didn't mean for all this to get so out of hand,' she began.

'Are we clear?' he repeated in the voice he used on mine sites.

She trembled, visibly intimidated for the first time.

Nik could see the struggle in her face and his anger evaporated in a wink.

He'd spent the night with some fairly explicit sexual fantasies about this woman, and this morning he'd learned a lot of things that didn't make him very happy with her. It wasn't a particularly good mix.

'I understand perfectly,' she said, swallowing hard, making it clear with her eyes she didn't.

Unlike the last woman throwing ultimatums at him like plates, a Spanish model who had apparently never heard the word no before, Sybella Parminter didn't really seem to understand the way this was played. If she backed down, he'd give her a break. She wasn't backing down.

It was disconcerting because he'd just discovered he didn't like her looking bewildered and upset.

For the second time. Because of him.

He stepped towards her.

'Mummy!' A small person flew out of the house and wrapped herself around Sybella's legs.

Mummy?

Six years widowed. He wasn't good with kids' ages but this one fitted the time span. Sybella was immediately scooping her up, the little girl wrapping her arms and legs around her mother like an octopus.

'This is your daughter?' he said redundantly.

'Yes.' She turned away to go into the house and the child cast a look over her mother's shoulder at him as if he were an ogre in a fairy tale. She stuck out her tongue.

Nik found himself staring at a blue door shut in his face and with the uneasy suspicion he'd made a mistake.

CHAPTER SIX

SYBELLA DROVE AS fast as she was legally able along the familiar road from Middenwold Town Hall where she worked on Fridays, back into Edbury.

In a panic from work she'd rung and let Mr Voronov know she was coming and that she was bringing the letters.

Beside her on the passenger seat was the box of letters that would clear her name.

She didn't want to be responsible for a further breach between grandfather and grandson because family was important, but she didn't see that she had much choice. She couldn't put her kindly impulses towards Mr Voronov above the risk to her future professional reputation if her activities at Edbury Hall were publicly condemned.

She switched on her hands-free phone device as Meg's name came up and her sister-in-law's excitable voice filled the car.

'I can't believe you've got one in the village!'

Sybella cursed silently. If Meg had heard about it down in Oxford, it must be all over the village.

'We lay traps and snares and catch them that way,' she responded drolly, although she was in *so much trouble* it was no longer funny.

'What'd you use?' said Meg wryly. 'A net?'

'No, the possibility of a lawsuit.' Sybella breathed in through her nose and out through her mouth and told herself she shouldn't drive and panic.

'I don't think that's your main problem. So Nik Voronov actually stepped off his boat and onto dry land.'

'Boat? What boat?'

'His billion-foot-long superyacht—all Russian oligarchs have them. They live on them.'

'Where do you get this from?'

'I have my sources. I also have other sources. According to the village grapevine, the two of you were throwing some serious sparks last night.'

Oh, yes, there had been sparks, but they had definitely fizzled. Then a new fear gripped her. 'What do you mean "the village grapevine"?'

'Syb, *everyone* knows. I've had three phone calls and Sarah was banging on Mum's back door at seven o'clock this morning wanting to know if it was true you were having sex up against a SUV in the car park at Edbury Hall last night. With *a man*.'

'Well, of course I'd be having sex with a man,' Sybella huffed impatiently, even as she recoiled from the idea her mother-in-law knew. 'Not that I was, mind, I was just… holding onto him—and Sarah's been cutting my hair for five years. She should know me better.'

'You're missing the point. To half the village this morning you're just an exhibitionist floozy—Sarah's on board with that, by the way—but everyone else thinks you're legitimately on together. They think he's your boyfriend.'

'What?'

'It explains why you were able to get the Hall opened again with so little fuss.'

Sybella's mouth fell open.

'Now's not the time to panic,' advised Meg. 'This guy owes you—after everything you've done for his grandfather, and now he's compromised your reputation.'

'I doubt he sees it that way,' Sybella said, gripping the steering wheel and wondering how floozy was going to translate at the pony club and how she would navigate that with Fleur. Her friends were too little, but their mothers were not.

'He's closing down the house to the public, Meg. He came over and told me this morning. He warned me off ever going near the place again.'

'He came to your *house*?'

'He was very angry with me.' Sybella took a breath and swallowed to avoid sounding as vulnerable as she felt. 'Up until then I thought I could persuade him to keep the place open, appeal to his better nature.'

'Good luck with that.' But Meg was oddly quiet for a moment and Sybella got the impression she'd given something away. 'You like him, don't you?'

'No, don't be silly. He's not my type at all. He's—he's bearish.'

'Well, remember what Goldilocks did in the original fairy tale? She jumped out of a window never to be seen again.'

By the time she reached the Hall, parked and made her way across the crunching gravel, Sybella wished she could leap out of that proverbial window. She was also praying she'd find Mr Voronov alone. What if Nik had heard the boyfriend gossip? She wouldn't be able to look him in the eye after that. Although she guessed, when it came to the court case, it would be his barrister who was asking the questions…

So much depended on Nik Voronov being reasonable. Reasonable! She was so sunk.

Sybella was shown inside and as she reached the open sitting-room door she could hear male voices. Her knees gave out a little and she wondered if she could just leave the box of letters here and run…

'She has a kid. You could have mentioned it, Deda.'

'How was I to know you would take this much interest?' Mr Voronov sounded amused, his rich accent rolling the 'r's.

Sybella ventured a little closer.

'Nor did you mention the husband.'

'She's a widow. She was barely married when the poor boy's van was hit by an oncoming car. It's a sad story.'

'One you fell for hook, line and sinker.'

Sybella stiffened.

But Mr Voronov still sounded amused. 'Your cynicism will not win her over, my boy.'

Win her over?

'I'm realistic, and you, old man, need to stay still or this is going to hurt.'

Sybella didn't know what she expected to find as she came abruptly into the room but it more than niggled that if his eldest grandson was overprotective when it came to his legal rights, it wasn't translating into the kind of care the elderly man deserved.

What confronted her wasn't an angry Nik Voronov bullying his grandfather, but the younger man hunkered down in front of his grandfather's chair, deftly applying ointment to the abscess above his ankle.

'Sybella, *moy rebenok*, this is a surprise. Come and sit down. My grandson is looking after me today.'

'So I see.' It was not a surprise; she'd rung ahead to let him know she was coming. So now she was feeling a little set up.

Only Nik looked just as taken aback as she felt.

'What are you doing here?' he growled.

'Nikolai!'

'I've brought biscuits.' She held up the tin. 'My mother-in-law made them and sends her regards.'

'You didn't whip them up yourself in between all the dusting and vacuuming?' This was from Nik, who continued to lay a gauze strip over the wound and tape it up.

Sybella couldn't help noticing he was utterly competent at the task. It didn't exactly fit her image of him as the absent grandson. Clearly he'd done this more than once.

'I would, if I whipped them up at midnight,' she said, not sure of her footing here. 'My mother-in-law doesn't work. I do.'

Nik straightened up and Sybella was reminded all over again of his physical presence and how it could fill the room. He was entirely too dominant for her peace of mind.

It would probably be better for everyone if he left the village today, and quickly.

Only she kept remembering how his hands had felt against her skin, how gentle he'd been drying her hair and later kissing her, making all the lights turn on and leaving them on.

'Nikolka, I think you should take Sybella to lunch.'

'Oh, no, that's not why I'm here.' Sybella stumbled in her haste over the words and she knew she sounded rude but it was excruciating to think Nik might feel obligated to sit through lunch with her.

'I just wanted to deliver the biscuits—' she reached into her handbag '—and these. The letters you sent me, Mr Voronov, in your grandson's name.' She put them down on his side table. 'I would appreciate it if you showed him the documentation I gave you. He might be a little kinder on all of us.'

She glanced up at Nik, who was now standing dangerously close to her. Her whole body was vibrating like a tuning fork. She had to get out of here!

'This just proves we were in a correspondence, or rather I was with your grandfather, and everything I did was above board.' She couldn't look him in the eye or she'd lose all her courage.

'What have you been saying to her, Nikolka?'

'Nothing he didn't have a right to—given he had no idea what was going on.'

She went over and crouched down, putting a hand on

Mr Voronov's arm. 'I understand why you did it, but it's caused me a deal of trouble and upset your grandson.'

The elderly man covered her hand with his own. 'You cannot blame an old man for trying.'

Sybella rather thought she could, but she wouldn't.

'You really need to sort this out with your grandson, but whatever happens with the Hall, I'll continue to bring Fleur here for stories. That won't change.'

She glanced a little furtively at Nik, who looked as if he was about to say something, and straightened up, making her way to the door. Every step felt awkward but she couldn't be in this room a moment longer with Nik Voronov looking at her like that.

Sybella was almost at her car when she heard his heavy crunching footsteps.

'Sybella, we need to clear a few things up.'

'There's nothing to clear up.' Sybella tried not to sound breathless, a little dismayed at how everything female in her sat up to pay attention. 'We don't have anything more to discuss.'

He looked down at her as if he didn't agree.

'You know everything now,' she said in a tight voice. 'I'm pretty much an open book, as you can see.'

She thrust her chin at the small cigar box he carried in his hand.

'Let me drive you back to town,' he said.

'I'm perfectly capable of looking after myself, thank you very much.'

'You haven't done a very good job so far,' he said bluntly. 'You should have spoken up for yourself earlier.'

'Right. Good to know for future reference, but, if you hadn't noticed, I was thinking of your grandfather.'

She dipped her head as a tremor ran through her and without a word Nik put his arm around her.

It wasn't an invasive gesture, he was just there, and it

felt so good she found herself with her face against his shoulder, taking a few sustaining breaths because she had to end this in a moment. She couldn't be doing this with this man.

'I meant to me,' he said quietly against her ear. 'You should have spoken up for yourself to me.'

'Why?'

'Because I like to get my own way. But I'm human, Sybella. I could have got this wrong.'

She stilled.

'Besides,' he said, 'what was I supposed to do? Let this all slide? I had to get to the bottom of it. I owe my grandfather a duty of care.'

'No, of course.' Breathing deeply, Sybella extricated herself and he let her go.

She'd seen how tender he'd been with his grandfather, the bond between them. It made her feel graceless for her critical words to him. She'd clearly understood very little. And Nik was…well, overwhelming her. Sybella allowed that thought in for the first time. She guessed it was only to be expected. He felt so solid and dependable and she was so tired of being the solid and dependable one, and, besides, he made her feel like a desirable woman.

She couldn't remember Simon ever making her feel this way. Loved, yes. Cared for. But not this pulsing, breathless awareness every time he came near her.

She gave him a quick upward look. 'I should go.'

She opened her car door. He held it while she climbed in, but the hand she extended to reach for the ignition was shaking badly.

Nik knew this was down to him. He had this out-of-character urge to reassure her. He couldn't stand it that her lips were mashed together and seeing that tremor in her hand had him wanting to put his arms around her again, but she was clearly embarrassed.

Instead he said gruffly, 'I'll drive you—that way you won't end up parked up a tree.'

To his surprise she didn't argue. She let him take the keys with another subdued 'thank you'. He walked her around to open the passenger door.

'You have amazing manners,' she said, looking a little shy now. 'I guess it's a Russian thing.'

'*Net*. It's my grandfather's thing.'

'You are close to him, aren't you?' she said when he got in the other side.

'He raised me from the age of nine.'

She was looking at him curiously as he adjusted her driving seat to accommodate his long legs. 'I didn't know that.'

He never spoke about his childhood or his relationship with Deda to anyone, but there was something about Sybella that consistently had him relaxing his guard.

'They had a summer house on the Baltic. There were cherry trees along the drive so in spring it was like a tunnel of pink and white petals, and in summer Deda would take me sailing the fjords.'

'It sounds idyllic.'

He shrugged. 'It was a haven of sorts.'

'From what?'

'Boarding school.'

'We have something in common,' she said.

'I know.' He named the elite public girls' school she'd attended and then regretted it because she went stiff as a board again. 'I did a little basic research on you this morning.'

'Research?'

'You're in my grandfather's life. I have to check you out.'

She sighed. 'I guess so. What did you find out?'

'Don't worry, I didn't have your taxes hauled over.'

'I didn't know anyone could do that. Search into someone's background that easily.'

'It's just basic facts anyone could find on your social media page.'

'I'm not on social media.'

'No.'

'Then how—?' She broke off and shook her head. 'Don't bother, you're rich, you have your ways.'

'You probably know just as much about me from the Internet.'

'I know you have a big mine in the Urals. I looked it up. It looks like a vast crater.'

'You can see it from the moon,' said Nik.

'I won't ask you if you have a problem with your ego,' she murmured, and for the first time a small smile tipped up one corner of her mouth.

'I didn't dig it all myself,' he responded, trying not to get too distracted by the sudden desire to make her smile some more, 'but, yeah, my ego is pretty healthy.'

She exhaled a soft crumpled laugh and looked away, her cheeks a little flushed.

Nik couldn't rip his eyes off her.

'Your little girl,' he coaxed, 'what's her name?'

Her expression instantly softened. 'Fleur.'

'It's a pretty name.'

'My little flower,' she said.

'How old is she?'

'Five and a half.'

'I didn't mean to scare her,' he said, the words feeling outsized, almost as if he was blundering again.

'You didn't scare her. She's just not used to raised voices.'

'Yeah, I deserve that.'

She eyed him almost shyly and again he got the impression Sybella wasn't anywhere near as tough as she pretended to be—or maybe needed to be. 'Your grandfather is teaching her to read. On Thursdays, when I'm here to take tours. Afterwards Fleur and I have tea with him.'

And he had forbidden her to come to the Hall again. He wanted to ask her why she hadn't let him know this earlier, but then he knew he hadn't given her much of a chance.

He was revisiting every hard thing he'd said to her since they'd met. He was beginning to think Sybella Parminter didn't really want anything from anyone, she was so determined to do it all herself.

'What I said about the house. I'm not here to ruin your or your daughter's relationship with my grandfather.'

She nodded, focused on some point outside the car.

'But I can't have my grandfather's home turned into…'

'A theme park, I know, I heard you.'

He had a strong urge to pull her into his arms, but that wasn't going to go down well.

'Mr Voronov talks a lot about his grandsons.' She looked over at him as if trying to read his face. 'He—he seems very proud of both of you.'

'Possibly simply relieved the two of us have managed not to break any laws or tarnish the family name,' Nik said, the brief smile he gave her almost boyish, and Sybella's heart did a stumble. 'He's not the robust man he once was. When my grandmother Baba died it was sudden and unexpected. We were all left floundering.'

Sybella suspected Nik was including himself in that floundering and her susceptible heart did more than stumble, it completely softened.

'Deda went overnight from the man who adapted to anything to how he is now, sometimes querulous and unhappy and mostly set in his ways.'

Sybella privately acknowledged the older man could be difficult, but she suspected it was because he felt managed. 'Mr Voronov has spoken to me of his wife.'

'Baba was everything to him.' And perhaps to her grandson, Sybella thought, watching a sadness weight his expression.

'Why did he come here of all places?'

'His health required visits to a clinic in London. I found myself with no choice but to accommodate his wish to not live in the city. He was in a hospital bed when he put a copy of *Country Life* in front of me and pointed out the photograph of Edbury Hall, and I hadn't been in a position to say no.'

'But you wish you had now.'

He was silent for a moment and then said quietly, 'No, things have changed since I arrived yesterday. It's not that clear-cut any more.'

Sybella told herself he wasn't referring to her but it was difficult to hold his gaze when he looked at her like that.

Nik watched the shyness she worked so hard to keep hidden soften her features, her hands working nervously in her lap.

'I don't suppose we can sit here all day,' she said, 'or is that your intention?'

Nik laughed and she appeared taken aback, as if his amusement was something slightly shocking. Was he that bad?

'Where do you want to go?'

He expected her to say back to work, but she looked out across the gravel courtyard and said, 'I've got a window of an hour before I need to pick Fleur up. Why don't we just go for a drive?'

There was a wash of colour in her cheeks again. He knew he couldn't start anything with her, but it couldn't hurt to take a drive.

'Why don't we?' he said and started the engine.

Sybella directed him to Linton Way Forest and they parked under the oaks. She got out and they walked down the overgrown walking track that famously weaved in and over the hills.

She told him about the uses the village had for the estate, and he listened.

'We have tours on Thursday afternoons. People are free to look at the west wing on weekends. The pony club use the grounds once a month for the gymkhana. That's about it so far. It doesn't impact on your grandfather's private life in the house. In fact he often appears unannounced to talk to tourists himself.'

'What I'm more interested in is the financial benefit to your little organisation.'

Sybella looked genuinely surprised.

'The Heritage Trust is a charity. Any money goes back into preservation—no one is pocketing it. We all volunteer.'

Nik reached around to massage the back of his neck and Sybella tried not to ogle his biceps. She was aware of him physically in a way that was making it difficult to concentrate on the serious matters they were discussing.

Although something had changed between them, Sybella just couldn't put her finger on what it was. He was more willing to listen and she was incredibly conscious of him physically.

'How did you come to be involved with them?'

'I have a degree and a diploma in archives management I earned part time when Fleur was younger. I needed some work experience and the Heritage Trust is all that's available in the area so I volunteered. That was three years ago.'

'That can't have been easy with a baby.'

'No.' She slanted a shy look his way, because it was nice to have that acknowledged. Encouraged, Sybella plunged into the tough stuff. 'I met your grandfather when the trust approached him about opening the house. He took an immediate dislike to our president but he was rather taken by Fleur, who was with me, and invited the two of us to tea. I do tours now on Thursdays for various schools and Fleur and I take tea with your grandfather afterwards. It's become a sort of ritual between us.'

'He talks about you a great deal.'

Sybella chewed on her lip. 'Nice things, I hope.'

'Nice being the word. He wants me to settle down with a nice girl.'

Oh, yes, she'd seen those girls on the Internet.

'The thing is, Sybella, I work hard,' he said unexpectedly.

She could have told him she worked hard too, but she guessed he and the rest of the world put more value on his work.

She watched those long lashes sweep down, the irony in his voice only making him seem more impenetrable, and Sybella could absolutely see why very beautiful, sought-after women would make an attempt at breaching all that male beauty and privilege with the aim of being the one to stick up her flag.

'I don't have time to invest in someone else's life. I date women with a corresponding world view.'

Sybella just kept nodding because she wasn't sure why he was telling her this.

'My grandfather doesn't approve,' he said dryly.

'He's very good with Fleur. I guess he wants great-grandchildren.'

Which was when it all fell neatly into place.

'Oh, no,' she said.

'Exactly. You knew nothing of this?'

'It simply didn't occur to me.'

'You do fit the criteria,' he said, with a slight smile that had Sybella's head snapping around in astonishment. 'He told me you would cook, clean and be a wonderful mother to our children,' he added.

But not Nik's criteria. Beautiful and not looking for— what did he call it—an investment? Sybella wrinkled her nose. It was a horrible term. The antithesis of an emotion.

He was talking about his grandfather's criteria.

Which she guessed were somewhat less exacting. To do with being a mum and a homebody. What would he say if she told him she'd never planned to take on any of this, it was life in its infinite surprises that had laid down those roles for her?

That she still, deep down, thought of herself as the independent individualist she had always been.

Did he really think she was angling herself at him?

'I didn't stand around in the courtyard last night waiting for you because your grandfather put me up to it!'

'Good to know.'

So that was what this romantic walk in the woods was all about.

She was being given the message he wasn't interested. He clearly thought she needed that message. Sybella's stomach hollowed out.

Probably now was a good time to sort this, when her ego was still reverberating from his direct hit and she was feeling a bit numb.

'There's just one small problem I should probably alert you to before we go our separate ways,' she said with as much dignity as she could muster. 'After the other night a lot of people in the village think you're my boyfriend.'

'Boyfriend?'

Sybella could feel herself turning pink. This was possibly one of the more embarrassing moments of her life.

'It's not what you think. I haven't rushed about telling people you are.'

'I'm not thinking that,' he said slowly.

'The other night at the Hall when you were holding me, some of the committee members got the wrong idea.'

She looked up at him, biting the inside of her lower lip. 'It will blow over, but I thought you should be made aware of it.'

Nik did his best to repress his amusement. He cleared his throat. 'People do jump to some out-there conclusions.'

'I know, crazy, right?' Sybella began to talk faster, because now they were at the more awkward bit, but she had to ask. 'There's one other thing. There aren't many opportunities in the immediate countryside for curatorial jobs, and my CV isn't exactly bursting at the seams, and if it gets out what happened with the house being open to the public on false pretences and you shutting things down, I can't see anyone ever hiring me. Ever.'

'I see.'

'Reputation matters in this business.'

'Makes sense.'

'If you could see your way clear to not pressing any legal charges—'

'Sybella, I didn't have all the information to hand. I'm not going to make your life any more difficult than it already is.'

'Oh.' She said a silent prayer. 'Thank you. You're not nearly as scary as you pretend to be, are you?'

It was his turn to look vaguely bemused.

'I don't mean to offend you,' she rushed on, 'but you can be a bit intimidating. I suppose it's because you're so big.'

'There's that,' Nik drawled, not sure if she knew how adorable she looked babbling at him as if he had feelings to hurt and she was worried about having stepped on them. 'I also have a lot of financial clout. You'd be amazed, Mrs Parminter, how the world works.'

'I suppose I would,' she said, blushing. 'I should probably get up to speed on that.'

He almost idly wound the end of one of her ringlets around his index finger before releasing it. It was a gesture implying intimacy, touching her but not quite touching her, which made her think about when they had touched, when they'd kissed.

'No, don't do that,' he said. 'Stay the way you are.'

'Too tall, too opinionated, too fat,' she blurted out.

Oh. God. Where had that come from? Because there was nothing more attractive to a man than a woman who bemoaned her looks. At least in some far-flung universe they didn't currently occupy.

To forestall any opinion he might have about her round body or her interest in him, she bowled on, 'Sorry, I don't know where that came from. I guess all those women you date don't go on about their looks because they're so gorgeous it doesn't occur to them.'

Sybella took a breath and stared in disbelief into the middle distance.

There was this awful silence. She wondered if he'd think it was odd if she just ran off at this point, screaming, into the forest.

Instead she made a swipe of her watch under her long sleeve.

'Oh, goodness, is that the time? I have to pick up Fleur from communal play. She's got a birthday party tomorrow with her little friends. She's taking fairy bread, and I still have to pick up the ingredients.'

She didn't wait for his response but started hurrying away from him, back towards the car.

'Listen to me babbling,' she threw over her shoulder. 'You don't mind me driving, do you?'

His steady tread on the gravel mocked her hasty, messy retreat. She climbed in the car and waited, clammy with horror. Although he'd told her she wasn't his type, he knew now, if he hadn't already suspected, she was besotted with him.

CHAPTER SEVEN

SYBELLA SAT CROSS-LEGGED on her sofa, looking into the inquisitive brown eyes of her daughter's house rabbit.

'I committed the cardinal sin,' she told Dodge. 'I exposed every last one of my frailties in front of Nik Voronov. I may as well have told him no one has seen my good lingerie except the wash bag in the machine in six years.'

She answered herself with a question. 'Can you get more specific there, Syb?'

'I told him I was fat and lonely and pretty much desperate.'

'Why would you do that?'

'Because he probably dates glamazons and his grandfather wants him to date me instead and he basically told me that wasn't going to happen and I sort of went…crazy.'

'Well, you do go a bit weird with a full moon.'

'I don't think it was the full moon, although given not only am I talking to a rabbit, I'm doing the voice so he answers back, it might be. And now I'm not even talking to the rabbit, I'm talking to myself. I am so screwed.'

'I wouldn't say that,' said a deep voice and Sybella almost fell off the couch.

Standing in the doorway off the hall was her Viking god.

'How did you get in?'

'You left the front door unlocked and I heard voices. I used that bell-pull. Are you aware it doesn't work?'

Sybella's cheeks felt red hot, mainly because she'd been caught making an idiot of herself. In front of the one person in the world she couldn't bear to think any worse of her.

'I'm sorry but you can't just walk in here.' She eased herself off the sofa carefully, not wanting to alarm Dodge, who was now sitting up, peering at Nik, ears aquiver.

'You even apologise to intruders into your home,' he said as if she'd revealed some secret about herself, then a look of amusement crossed his face. 'Is that rabbit for real?'

'His name is Dodge, and he's a house rabbit, there's another one around, so please keep your voice down.'

'I wouldn't want to frighten the woodland creatures,' he said, lowering his voice, looking at her in a way that made Sybella weirdly think he was including her in that. He closed the door gently behind him so that suddenly her living area felt very small.

'What are you doing here?'

'I came to say goodbye. I'm leaving in the morning.'

Sybella was hit by a punch of utter disappointment. He was leaving? 'Oh.'

He wore a T-shirt and jeans, as casual as she'd seen him, only on him it looked like one of those ads in a glossy magazine where the guy was glowering sullenly at the viewer and toting some serious machismo, and usually there was a dangerous-looking motorcycle behind him. Yes, Nik Voronov appeared to have stepped out of those pages into her living room.

And he'd come to say goodbye?

'I read your proposal about opening the gatehouse as a tourist hub for the house and estate.'

Sybella was so busy swimming in disappointment he was leaving she didn't completely take it in.

''It's a sound proposal,' he said. 'I'm willing to talk about it.'

Now? This was good, he was staying—to talk about the Hall. It was a big step in the right direction—for the Hall.

Sybella did an internal eye roll. She really needed to get herself together around him.

'The truth is I'm under a bit of pressure with the old man.'

It wasn't what she expected to hear and it wiped all the nonsense in her head. He needed her help. He actually moved a hand over the back of his neck, the age-old posture of male admission he was willing to lay down arms. That alone spoke volumes about his feelings for his grandfather.

She melted. 'You really love him, don't you?'

He shrugged. 'He's my grandfather.'

Sybella thought of her lousy, self-interested parents and then shoved them back where they belonged, over a cliff and into the ocean of people who could break your heart if you let them.

'I'd like to speak to you about him, something personal. Can I sit down?'

He didn't wait for the invitation, but lowered himself onto the armchair, catty-corner from the sofa she was now inhabiting.

He leaned forward, resting his forearms over his broad knees, fixing her with that intent grey gaze.

She'd been entertaining so many romantic fantasies about this man over the last twenty-four hours, to have him in the flesh inhabiting her small living room had the quality of one of those.

'Where's your little girl?'

'Her aunty Meg is here for the weekend so she's having a sleepover with her at my parents-in-law's house. They live on the other side of the village.'

Something flickered in his gaze and Sybella could suddenly hear her heartbeat in her ears.

'You were going to tell me something…personal about you and your grandfather?' she prompted, aware her voice had a slightly airless quality to it.

He gave her a half-smile as if acknowledging the irony

of the 'something personal' when right about now everything about him being here felt personal.

'I am,' he said. 'It begins with my parents. They were childhood sweethearts, Darya and Alex, and had been together for a long time before they had a separation of about a year, and my mother got pregnant with me. She mustn't have thought that much of the guy because she rekindled her romance with Alex and he was apparently happy to call me his son.'

Sybella didn't know what to say.

'I don't have any memories of my mother. She had a rare kidney condition and died when I was still a baby. Papa raised me alone until he remarried. They were good years or so I'm told. I lived on a lot of film sets but this is in Russia. Alex always used the same people and the crew were like family. When I was five I got a very flashy stepmother and several months later a baby brother. Sasha. I'm sure you've heard about him.'

'Your grandfather mentions him from time to time. He seems to be in the public eye quite a bit.'

'My little brother is famous for his films and his parties, not always in that order,' Nik responded, but there was real warmth in his voice, as there had been when he'd spoken to his grandfather. Sybella was beginning to feel a little foolish about all her doubts. They were clearly a strong unit.

'Sasha was four years old when our father slipped on a ledge climb in Turkey. Papa was chasing a shot for a film he was putting together. He always took risks. My brother is very much like him.'

Nik's expression conveyed this wasn't necessarily a positive thing.

'I went to live with my grandparents after Alex's death. My grandfather was a successful businessman. I don't know if he's talked to you about that part of his life.'

'No, not really. We talk about family and books mainly.'

'His favourite subjects.' Nik was scrutinising her and she couldn't blame him. She was fast becoming the vault of Voronov family secrets.

'I'm not indiscreet, Nik. I won't talk about this to anyone.'

He smiled then. 'I wouldn't be sharing this with you if I thought you would. I'm telling you all this, Sybella, because it appears my grandfather has taken quite a shine to you, and he's told me how good you've been to him, and I behaved badly last night and I don't want to leave here with you thinking the worst of me.'

'But I don't,' she began, a little too anxious to assure him her feelings had changed. 'I saw how close the two of you are this afternoon.'

'I owe him so much,' Nik said simply. 'I only knew how much when I was fifteen and needed a blood transfusion and neither of my grandparents could help out. That was when Baba and Deda sat me down and told me the true state of affairs. I wasn't their grandson.'

'But you are,' said Sybella unbidden, and then flushed. 'I'm sorry, you don't need me to tell you that.'

'It's all right.' He was smiling at her and the effect of that smile was singing all over her body. 'So you see,' he said, 'we have something in common.'

'Have you tracked him down, your biological father?' She stopped, embarrassed. 'I'm sorry, that's another very personal question. You don't have to answer that.'

'No, I haven't met him.' He shifted and Sybella could see this weighed on him. 'I have his name. I haven't done anything about it. I don't know if I ever will.' He rolled those big shoulders. 'What about you? Have you gone looking for your real parents?'

Which was a neat way of diverting the conversation. Sybella wondered if he was even conscious of how everything in his body conveyed tension when he talked about his biological father.

'According to the records office, my father is unknown and my mother was a student who gave me up for adoption,' she answered. 'We got together when I was twenty. She came to my wedding. She remembers Fleur with birthday cards, which is something. I think it's hard for her to maintain relationships with people. She seems to have had a difficult life.' She looked down at her hands.

'I'm sorry I was dismissive about your adoptive parents the other night,' he said. 'I shouldn't have said what I did.'

She looked up. 'That's all right, it's forgotten.'

Nik was gazing back at her steadily, and this intimacy created by their mutual confessions was making Sybella feel something like the first steps in a friendship was springing up between them, only none of her friends were six-feet-six-inch Russians with Cossack eyes and a way of looking at her that made her think he might like to kiss her again.

'What a pair we make,' he said in that quiet, gravelly way of his.

Sybella dropped her gaze, suddenly immensely shy.

'What I guess I'm getting around to, Sybella, is that Deda has helped me through some difficult times as a kid, Baba as well. I owe them both a great deal. I'm cognisant I may have dropped the ball with Deda recently, but I want you to know he's in safe hands and why.'

Sybella blinked rapidly because she could feel ready emotional tears surging up.

Blast those pregnancy hormones. They'd arrived six years ago and never really gone away.

'I could see how close you were earlier today.' She dabbed at her eyes. 'I'm sorry if I implied anything else. I obviously didn't have the full picture and you weren't obliged to tell me. I mean, it's not as if we know one another.'

'I'd like to get to know you better.' His Russian accent was suddenly stronger and Sybella almost slid off the sofa again.

He would? Don't be stupid. He doesn't mean it like that.

'I would too.' She tried to think of something to avert attention from her burning cheeks. 'I can offer you something to eat. I was just going to mix up a stir-fry for dinner. Would you like some?'

Nik didn't hesitate despite having just eaten a full meal with his grandfather. 'Yes, I would.'

When she leaned forward to stuff her feet into slippers, as if to completely assure the direction of the evening, her breasts moved sumptuously against her top, giving him a glorious view of how generous Mother Nature had been.

'The kitchen's this way,' she said, straightening up as if nothing extraordinary had just happened, and with a shy smile she gestured for him to follow her.

Nik followed.

His gaze dropped to the fulsome curve of her bottom beneath the soft fabric of her drawstring pants. He'd never considered himself a connoisseur of the female bottom. But right now he was seeing the benefits of a woman with some heft in her pendulum. In fact he was pretty much transfixed by that sweet wobble and sway.

In the kitchen she had a bottle of Spanish red out on the counter.

'Can you get some glasses? They're in the cabinet over there,' she instructed as she began gathering her ingredients around her.

He found a couple of wine glasses and poured. He'd drunk worse.

Presently the place began to smell delicious from whatever was heating up on the stove.

Vaguely he remembered his grandfather mentioning Sybella's cooking skills, and he had to admit there was something about Sybella that made a woman being competent in a kitchen sexy.

He didn't do domestic scenes with women. He had a chef, or he ate out. His stepmother had been allergic to anything but restaurants, and until his grandparents had swept in and given him a home he'd eaten a lot of take-out.

So deep down he associated home cooking with stability and the love of his grandparents. But he wasn't one of those guys who clung to redundant gender roles. Which made this weird because underneath all that he was still the son of generations of conservative Russian males, and he really was enjoying watching Sybella cook for him.

'So you work at the town hall?'

'Yes.' She was busily chopping up apples but she gave him her shy smile. 'I'm the assistant archivist. You can find me in the basement with all the dusty files. We're putting a lot of things on the computer system but so much of what we handle is original documentation, dating back before the English Civil War, registers of births, deaths and marriages, land holdings, town maintenance. It's all there, and we keep the originals in the library for academics and the occasional documentary film maker. I chase things up for people three days a week.'

'This interests you, doesn't it, the past?'

'I like permanence,' she said, laying down the knife. 'It comforts me to know ten generations have lived here, in this house. People have been born here and died here, been married out of this house, triumphed and suffered and dreamed within its walls. I like old things, the way they soak up the lives of the people who have lived in them and with them.'

Nik remembered what she'd told him about being adopted, about being handed back, about her adoptive parents not being in her child's life.

This was important to her for good reasons. She'd pulled a bad hand as a kid, and, looking around her house, he could see she'd made more than a home with her daughter. She'd put down roots.

'So what plans did you have for the Hall before I bought it?'

She looked up in surprise, 'How did you know—?' She broke off and shook her head. 'You've been ahead of me all along, haven't you?'

'It's not difficult to work out.'

'Well,' she said, beginning to dice again, 'apart from turning the gatehouse into a tourist hub, we were planning on having open-day picnics in the grounds, but that was under the last owner. He was an American, you understand.' She cast an almost mischievous look at him through her lashes.

'Meaning a Russian is not big-spirited enough to get out of the way of English heritage?'

'No, no,' she said, laughing, and the sound arrested him. He'd never heard her laugh. 'I meant he knows the value of a buck. Edbury could be quite profitable.'

It was the last thing he'd expected Sybella to say, and he agreed with her. He'd been thinking along the same lines, but ruled a line under it. This was his grandfather's home; he wasn't dislodging him.

'It can't be done. Deda loves it here.'

Sybella put down the knife she was using with a clatter. 'Oh, my goodness, no, you misunderstand me. This wasn't my idea, it was your grandfather's.'

'Prostit?'

Sybella bit the inside of her lip. She was beginning to look forward to the moments when he spoke his language to her.

'Mr Voronov has been looking at literature from other local stately homes. We've been talking about what could be done here. To hold onto the heritage of the Hall to pass on to future generations. I thought you could be brought on board,' she said, then lowered her gaze because she was beginning to wonder if in a minute he'd warn her off going within twenty metres of the Hall again. 'We all care desperately about keeping the place historically intact for the future. And to be honest, Nik, I think it's given your grandfather a reason to get up in the mornings.'

Nik unfolded his arms. 'Why don't you tell me about it, then, your plans?'

'Truly?' she said.

Their eyes met and hers dropped first. She began dicing a little harder.

'Naturally it would take a lot of setting up. There are bylaws, not to mention the increase in traffic using local roads. We don't want the village being overrun by tourists. We get quite enough in the summer. Not so much Brits but busloads from overseas. Everybody wants to poke around in some between-the-wars version of England with its winding lanes and thatched cottages.'

'Says the woman who lives in one.'

She smiled and Nik felt something lodge behind his breastbone. This beautiful woman, who had blinked back tears when he'd told her about his parents, and dissolved in his arms the other night and now was preparing dinner for him, was smiling at him.

Those eyes stayed locked to his and he was suddenly only aware of the hard, heated consequences of being around her for the past twenty-four hours beating against the buttons on his jeans.

'Careful.' He laid a hand on hers where she was chopping up the apple. She looked down to see she'd almost nicked her finger. 'You're not paying attention,' he chided, stroking her finger with his thumb.

'No, I'm not,' she said with a small smile, those hazel eyes flitting to his shyly but with a look of unvarnished sexual yearning before they swooped down to his mouth, giving her away so entirely all he could do was remove the knife from her hand and wait for her eyes to lift again and dance to his.

He hadn't planned to make a move on her. He'd only known he owed her an explanation and an apology and the temptation of seeing her again had been too strong.

She had lowered her lashes and he was able to study her face, the boldness of her mouth, the soft, full curve of her cheeks. She was so damn lovely.

The heat from the pot had turned her cheeks pink and curled the fair tendrils escaping from her bun around her face. The fragrance of rosemary and basil, along with the olive oil from the pan, was on her fingertips and he was imagining those fingers touching his skin.

He wanted to lift her onto the bench, lay her down among her fresh ingredients and plunder her soft pink mouth until she was his.

'So your daughter is at her sleepover?' Nik heard himself ask as if they were having a general conversation.

Sybella nodded, not trusting her voice. She knew what the question meant. Telling him there was a fifty-fifty chance she'd get a phone call from Meg at around eleven and Fleur would want to come home would probably sink things where they stood.

She could surely keep these two halves of her life separate for an evening. He would be gone tomorrow and she would go back to keeping all those balls in the air.

But she didn't want to think about tomorrow. Just thinking about everything she had on her plate would surely close down her inner sex goddess completely.

She turned away from him abruptly and went over to the hob. She fumbled with the gas as she turned off the flame under the saucepan and pan, telling herself she could have this once. With this gorgeous man. Nobody needed to know.

Besides, it wasn't anyone's business…

Her breath caught as he put a hand around her waist and turned her and then laid a finger against her cheek and eased away an errant curl.

She gazed into his heated eyes and said, 'Maybe we can skip dinner.'

CHAPTER EIGHT

SHE TOOK HIS HAND, sliding her fingers along his, and he enfolded her slighter grasp within his own and she led him out of the kitchen into the narrow hall and to the foot of the stairs.

Nik saw a moment's hesitation in her, as she laid a foot on the first step and then stopped. Which was when he picked her up. She said something ridiculous about being too heavy but he'd already mounted the stairs and she was looking at him as if no man had acted like a Neanderthal around her, when he could imagine most of the men she met probably fantasised about doing this with her. But didn't make it past that first step. Her hesitation, the way she looked at him, told him this was not a regular occurrence in her life.

Her bedroom door was directly opposite the stairs and open. The double bed didn't look big enough but as he lowered her onto it he could see there was enough room for their purpose.

'Let me do this,' she said, before he could kiss her.

She was climbing up on her knees, tugging and pulling his T-shirt up over his head.

He was surprised by her willingness to take the initiative given her nervousness, but he wasn't complaining as he finished the job for her and tossed the T-shirt over his shoulder.

'I'm going to do this,' she said and he could have told her he wasn't going to argue.

She ran her fingers down his torso, exploring the defi- nition of his muscles and tendons beneath the skin intricately converging to form that V below his taut abdomen, undoing a few of the buttons on his jeans.

Nik's breathing was already coming in snags as he watched her explore him with her fingertips. Her touch was so light, the expression on her face transfixed.

'Is this okay?'

She foraged under those loose buttons, meeting his eyes. 'Yeah, that's okay,' he said, swallowing as she slowly slid her hand over the length of him.

Nik sucked in a breath and went still, eyes lambent, the breath hissing between his teeth as she explored him with her hand.

When she was sure he definitely hadn't had enough she smiled and removed her hand and then slowly, enticingly began to move that same hand over the button fly of his jeans, opening it up.

'Are you trying to kill me, *dushka*?' he half joked, his voice hoarsened with the effort.

'That would defeat our purpose, don't you think?' Somehow that combination of her shy smile and her knowing eyes as she tugged his jeans down over his lean hips, taking his boxers with them, had the same effect as her hand on his erection.

She came over him, measuring him with her eyes, and lowered her head, her hair sliding forward to curtain her face as she licked him from base to tip.

Nik hissed and gripped the coverlet, fisting it as he fought not to disgrace himself. He was on a hair trigger; just watching her was enough to set him off.

She'd been so shy.

He really hadn't expected this…this sex goddess.

He tried to control the building reaction to her lapping, swirling pink tongue, the graze of her plump lips, and as she slid him into her mouth he knew he wasn't going to make it if she went any further and he gently disengaged her and deftly rolled her back onto the bed.

She lay there, smiling up at him as if she'd accomplished something she was proud of, as she should be, her eyes glistening, her mouth wet, her breaths coming even shorter as he slid one finger into the vee of her soft cotton top, where it dipped into the valley between her breasts.

He went to strip her shirt off but she clamped her hands over his.

'The light,' she said, blinking anxiously at him as if he might say no.

He looked up at the overhead, a vintage frilled thing that was currently lighting things up to his satisfaction.

'It's in my eyes,' she said, looking suddenly oddly flustered. 'Can we have it off?'

Only an idiot would argue with her at this point. He bounded from the bed to turn the main light off. Sybella had reached across and switched on the lamp. The room was suddenly in shadows but Sybella was bathed in a diffused caramel glow.

She looked positively feline and possibly the most sensual creature he had ever laid eyes on.

'Anything else you want doing?' he asked, coming down beside her on the bed.

He ran his hands over her hips and behind to the curve of her generous bottom still clad in satin something and into her eyes crept a touch of tension. He snuffed it out by kissing her hungrily, devouring the soft, sweet mouth he'd been dreaming about for the last twenty-four hours.

He pushed her cotton top up over her breasts, lifting her arms and arching over her as he slid the cotton free. She was wearing a simple bra embroidered with pink forget-me-nots and with her flaxen hair tumbling over her shoulders she looked like every fantasy he'd ever had.

'*Bogu*, you're beautiful,' he said, sliding one strap off her shoulder.

'Am I?'

'Gorgeous.' He tried to imbue the assertion with some of the reverence he really did feel, but it wasn't easy when all he wanted to do was fall on her like a sex-starved teenager who'd never been this close to a naked woman's body in his life.

'You're a bona fide sex goddess,' he asserted and she responded by wrapping her arms around his neck and coming up to meet him.

As their mouths fused he was no longer able to keep up this song of seduction and skill; he was just a man a little clumsy with lust.

He slid his mouth down her throat, licking over her cleavage, feeling her shiver against him in anticipation. He reached under her and released the catch of her bra and then slowly, with an intensity of purpose because frankly her breasts deserved worshipping, he peeled her pretty cups away.

He took his time to look his fill, feeling her eyes on him, her rapid, short breaths telling him she found this thrilling too. He took one taut pink nipple between his lips and licked. She gasped and bucked under him. He moved from one breast to the other, licking and sucking and moulding her, listening to her sighs and the little noises she made.

He untied the drawstring on her pants and hooked his thumbs under the sides of her satin knickers on the way down and peeled them both off, his hands actually shaking. She'd left herself as nature made her, the soft fair curls at the apex of her thighs as pretty as anything he'd ever seen.

He traced the seam of her sex with his index finger and she gave a little 'oh' as he lowered himself to kiss her there and inhale the heady scent of aroused woman. He licked her without warning and then again and she cried out and pulsed to her first orgasm, but he didn't stop, he went on and on until he wrung the last glorious ripple from her.

When he lifted his head and looked up she had her eyes half closed, her hair spread around her, the sensuality of her on full uninhibited display, and satisfaction thundered through him. She gave him a dreamy smile.

'What a little honeypot you are,' he told her and placed a kiss on her lower belly, where she was softer and she had a silvery pale tributary of zigzagging lines and some pinkish ones that hadn't faded yet, if they ever would.

Sybella watched him through her lashes. She didn't mind those tiger stripes—her baby had given her those. He traced them with his tongue and kissed her belly again, coming up over her with intent.

'Not a honey trap any more?' Her voice was smoky with satisfaction.

His grin turned rueful. 'I take it I'm not forgiven for that.'

Sybella reached for him, her hands smoothing over the warm breadth of his chest to curl over his shoulders where the muscles were bunched. She couldn't get enough of his body. 'Oh, I think you're forgiven.'

'Happy?'

She gave him a sly smile. 'Not completely.'

'I still have some work to do—what could the lady possibly want from me now?'

He settled between her thighs and Sybella had a blissful moment of being exactly where she wanted to be with exactly the right man.

He'd seen her body now in all its opulent glory and she was beginning to think just maybe the awkwardness with Simon hadn't been entirely down to her, because at no point in any of this had she wanted to be covered by a sheet. Nik was obviously, unashamedly devouring her with his eyes.

She could feel him hard and impatient, stroking himself against her. *Right there.*

Sybella shifted her pelvis to bring him to her but he was pulling away.

No, no.

'Where are you going?' she asked incredulously.

'I need to suit up.'

Sybella flopped back on the mattress, grateful one of them was using their brain.

Nik had pulled a couple of condoms out of his wallet.

She gave him a lopsided smile. 'You were confident.'

'I had hopes.'

'Hurry,' she urged.

Nik discovered his hands were shaking slightly as he rolled one on and she moved to take over.

'You really are going to kill me,' he said between his teeth.

'Well, like I said before, that would defeat our purpose.' She said it with a little smile on her face that grew as she slid her hands over his hips, coming up on her knees and then looping her arms over his shoulders.

He spread his hands around her bottom, enjoying the give of her, the softness, the sheer female voluptuousness of her body against his harder frame.

He was against her and she made a soft little noise against his throat. Nik didn't need the encouragement and drove home, the sheer size of him paralysing her senses for a moment and then his mouth was hot at her neck and he was sheathed inside her and Sybella sighed her deep-felt appreciation, turning her mouth to his as he kissed her, smothered her mouth with his, before lowering his head to suck on her breasts, leaving her gasping.

He positioned her with his big hands and thrust again

and again and when he thought he couldn't hold back she climaxed around him, the intensity of it tipping him over the edge. Conscious thought was a long time coming and when it returned to Nik they were lying in each other's arms, her eyes soft and no longer as curious as they had been when he'd first looked into them in the snow last night. She had her answer.

'Well,' she panted, her breath soft against his shoulder, 'that was…something.'

'*Da*, something.' Too fast, too urgent, just…sensational. He felt grateful, dazed and looking forward to taking that trip to heaven again.

Soon.

He stroked the hair off her face, feeling an unaccountable level of well-being he hadn't felt in years. Her skin was dewy with faint perspiration, her cheeks pink; she was fairly glowing.

His gaze moved over the rounded shapes of her sumptuous breasts and flagrant hip curved under his hand. He squeezed her softly, enjoying the flesh under his hand.

'You like looking at me,' she said, her fingers tangling in his chest hair.

'I'd be crazy if I didn't.' He touched his lips to the tip of her nose and then her eyelids and finally her temple. Nothing salacious, more in reverence for how tender she made him feel.

'I like looking at you.' She massaged her lower lip with her teeth, as if something else was on her mind. 'I always had…trouble taking my clothes off in front of Simon. I felt, I thought, I don't know, I wondered what he saw.'

He gave her a lascivious smile and she smiled back and then her eyes filled and overflowed with tears.

'Sorry,' she gasped, cupping her face with her hands, 'so silly. Don't mind me.'

She was so English. So polite in the oddest circumstances. She was a woman. She was emotional. She shouldn't be ashamed of it. It made him feel tender. So he reached for her and kissed her tears and murmured to her in Russian, which seemed to quiet her. Presently her shoulders stopped quaking and she lay still against him.

'You were very young when you got married,' he said.

She nodded against his shoulder. 'Only I didn't think I was. I felt like I'd lived a lifetime before I met Simon.' She raised her face to look at him. 'He was my first love. We met in my first year at university. But after a year he—we—decided to take a break for the summer. He was going on a dig in Athens—amateur archaeology was his hobby, we kind of had that in common—but I couldn't go with him. I needed to work, save some money, so it was a break in our relationship.'

Nik waited; he suspected he knew where this was going.

'The next term he wanted to get back together but he told me he'd had a sort of a fling with another girl. It was okay,' she hurried on, glancing at him as if daring him to condemn her precious Simon. 'We were split when it happened.'

But he could hear in her voice there had been no splitting as far as Sybella was concerned. She was loyal. He'd known her twenty-four hours but he'd seen her loyalty in action, keeping the crucial information about the letters from him to protect Deda.

'Then, you see, she was in a few of my tutorial groups so I had to spend the rest of the year seeing her several times a month. I got a little funny about it. She never said anything, I don't think we ever exchanged any more than the normal pleasantries, but she must have known.'

'Do you want me to comment or just listen?' Nik had a number of thoughts, all of them about her fool of a husband.

'Listen, I think.' She gave a soft, nervous laugh. 'I've

said all the critical things in my head and I said a few to Simon at the time. It's just, we got back together—obviously—but I knew something wasn't right. Even on my wedding day there was this niggle.'

'He was still seeing her.'

'Gosh, no, no! Simon wasn't that kind of guy at all.'

Nyet, and in Sybella's partial eyes probably never would be. Nik did his best not to take a dislike to her dead husband.

'He was very ethical. I mean, he didn't have to tell me.'

Nik wisely kept his own counsel. But the thought remained, I wouldn't have told her, I would have protected her from the knowledge. Then the next startling thought arrived: I wouldn't have gone to another woman.

Not when the girl was Sybella. She seemed to him a little traditional, the kind of woman who would expect fidelity. If the guy had loved her, he would have known that.

She eyed him, nervous once more. 'I know this will sound silly but I got a bit funny about my body. I got it into my head Simon didn't find me desirable.' She frowned a little, as if puzzling over the girl she'd been.

Now Nik officially wanted to punch her dead husband.

'You see, this other girl, she was very pretty and she was tiny, like a fairy tiny, and I'm not.'

Nik didn't know what to do with that. 'No, you're not,' he said.

She shoved him. 'You're not supposed to say that.'

He nudged up her chin to look at her, so incredibly lovely with her light-in-a-forest eyes and her pale pre-Raphaelite curls tumbling over her shoulders and those gorgeous breasts, and he knew in that moment what all men knew: they would never understand women.

'Listen, Lady Godiva, my interest in fairies ended around about the age of four. I want a woman in my bed, and I want her soft and warm and capable of giving as good as she gets—in and out of bed. Your Simon was young, yes?'

'Twenty-two when we got married.' Sybella's voice was soft and she was looking at him hopefully, as if he might say the very thing that was going to fix all this for her.

Nik wasn't so sure. He knew from personal experience how deep resentments could shoot those roots when they attached young. Rejection by your parents had to leave deep fault lines, and Sybella had just admitted hers. To him. As if he was worth her trust. But to respond in kind was something he couldn't do.

So he took hold of the surface problem and strangled the life out of it for her.

'I'd pretty much sussed it by twenty-two,' he said, meeting her eyes, 'but it can take some men a lifetime. Whatever package it comes in, Sybella, it's the woman inside who makes you notice her, who reduces you to an idiot and has you promising all kinds of things just to get her naked.'

Her mouth had fallen open slightly in the same way it had when he'd swooped her up into his arms earlier this evening and carried her up here.

Then her eyes began to kindle.

'You didn't promise me anything,' she said in a low voice.

He grinned at her. 'You should have asked, *dushka*.'

She was clearly trying not to smile.

'You're just saying that because you think it will get you laid again.'

'*Da*, there is that.'

The wounded vulnerability in her eyes had been replaced by the light he'd seen earlier.

That light was like a lighthouse beam guiding him right back to her and all that female lusciousness deep down she must know drove men mad.

'So how about it?'

And her mouth, which had become an instrument of both torture and pleasure to his body, curved up in a smile, carving that dimple deeply.

Bogu, he wanted to kiss that sweet mouth.

But she tucked her hand behind his neck again and brought his mouth down to where she wanted it, on her breasts.

Yeah, he'd died.

This was heaven.

CHAPTER NINE

SOMETHING GAVE A CRACK and the bed lurched to one side and then another crack and the headboard came away from the iron frame.

Nik sprang out of bed and, saying something in Russian, went around and checked out the situation.

'Should I get out?' she asked, not wanting to move in case it all collapsed.

'Hold still,' he grunted. 'I'll fix this.'

She gave a soft shriek as he dislodged the mattress base from the rest of the frame and Sybella found herself staring up at a ceiling that was significantly farther away than it had been a moment ago.

Nik carried the iron base in its two pieces out into the hall and leaned it up against the wall. Sybella watched him, craning her neck.

'You don't have to go, do you?' she called. 'The bed still works.'

Sybella screwed shut her eyes. *The bed still works?* Why didn't she say *I still work* and be done with it?

When Nik came back into the room he sized up the bed and then lowered the lean strength of his magnificent male body down beside her.

He shifted on the mess of twisted sheets and Sybella was suddenly very conscious of the lack of space in general, of how absurd this situation was in her small bedroom where she'd spent the last six years being nothing more than a harried working mum with no head space for what had happened here now.

No, space at the moment was definitely at a premium.

His eyes were like dark onyx in the available light from

the steadily burning lamp, and Sybella could see herself reflected in them but in a way she'd never really viewed herself before. This wanton creature who had revelled in her seduction of this powerful man, whom she'd pretty much brought to his knees—literally given a couple of the positions he'd held her in.

'I have to say, *dushka*,' he said in a gravelly voice, 'leaving is the last thing that's on my mind.'

He propped himself up, those big shoulders rising over her like cliffs, making it impossible to see over or around him, and Sybella found herself sinking under him again because this old bed, despite being a double, was really not made for two when one of them was six feet six. She enjoyed, however, that sensation of being rendered small and delicate and in thrall to him.

'You shouldn't have dragged me up here if you didn't want me to stay the night.'

'What do you mean I dragged you up here?'

'Lured me, then.' He gave her that slow, sexy smile and laid a kiss on her shoulder, her collarbone, the slope of her right breast, grazing dangerously close to her nipple. Little traitors sat up. She shivered as he brushed the underside of his unshaven jaw over one.

'You look like a wanton dairymaid—how could I resist?'

'Is that a reference to the size of my breasts?'

'*Da,*' he chuckled, brushing his lips over them, 'and your blonde hair and your dimples—and your roomy arse.'

'My what?' She hit his chest playfully as he slid his hands under her.

'More to get a grip on.' He laughed, doing just that. She'd never been more proud of her wide, womanly behind.

Then a thought hit her. 'I just imagined you'd be wanting to get back to your superyacht or whatever.'

He studied her. 'Superyacht?'

'Meg, my sister-in-law, has this theory that's where all the rich Russians live.'

'You've been talking about me?'

'Everyone in the village is talking about you.'

'I'm only interested in what you had to say.'

Sybella stroked his chest in seemingly idle circles. 'I said you weren't very happy with me.'

'I'm happy with you now.' He gave her bottom a squeeze.

She gave him a gentle shove.

'My yacht is about this big.' He measured it out to about an inch between his thumb and forefinger.

Sybella couldn't help it. 'Lucky for me that's only your yacht.'

'I could show it to you some time.'

'I thought you already had.' He smothered her giggle with a kiss and her blood began to hum again.

'I also have another estate in Northumbria,' he murmured against her mouth, and he named it and Sybella went a little pale.

'That's one of the finest castles in the north.'

'Too far and too cold,' he dismissed.

Sybella sat up, dislodging the sheet in her surprise. 'Then why did you buy it?'

'Tax purposes.'

'If you keep buying up my nation's history at this rate I'll end up working for you.'

'Would that be so bad?' He traced a line from her collarbone to her nipple. 'If we could keep doing this.'

Sybella's breath stuttered in her chest and not just because her breasts felt sensitive and responsive to him. Did he think they could find a way to keep doing this?

'Any more grand estates I should know about?' she asked, pulling at the sheet to cover herself again.

'No, just the two.' He kissed the exposed slope of one

breast and then the other, dislodging the covers so he could look at her while he played with them. Sybella was put in mind of a boy with a new toy.

'Real estate in London is more profitable. Russia isn't the safest place to keep all your eggs—' he spread his hands to cup either side of her breasts '—so I've got other baskets.'

Then mercifully he stopped talking about real estate and concentrated on their mutual pleasure.

When she opened her eyes hours later it was light. Nik was pulling on his shirt, and she sat up on her elbows, dragging the covers with her.

'What time is it?' She yawned.

'Almost nine.'

'I guess you should go,' she said half-heartedly.

'I should go,' he concurred.

He was looking down at her as if he still wanted her and Sybella's ego swelled a little more than it should, along with the plummeting feeling she was going to have to let him go and there didn't seem to be a clear-cut path for them, assuming he wanted one.

'When will you be back? In Edbury, I mean.'

Nik began reattaching his watch.

'I was thinking I could fly you up to London next weekend, if you could arrange someone to look after your daughter.'

Fly her up to London? She'd been thinking more along the lines of, When are you coming back to Edbury to see your grandfather? Maybe we could have dinner… Although given they'd already plunged in at the deep end dinner was always going to end here. So maybe London was the right option.

Only it sounded so illicit. And at the same time he was making plans for them, they didn't involve him stepping into her world, and she was a little taken aback by the impression he saw her daughter as an impediment.

'Fleur,' she said uncomfortably. 'Her name is Fleur.'

He smiled but he didn't say her name and a little part of Sybella curled at the edges like blight on a rose leaf.

'I guess I could come up to London. The thing is, I'm really only comfortable with Fleur staying with her aunty Meg or her grandparents, and I can't be away from her for more than a night. She's still so little…'

Sybella trailed off. He was getting out his phone. She guessed he wasn't really that interested in the logistics. It was her domestic life—not his.

He finished buttoning his shirt.

'Where's your phone?'

But he'd already spotted the chair in the corner where her soft patchwork carryall was slumped. Her phone lay on top of it.

She climbed out of bed, wrapping herself in the pale gold blanket, and drew close behind him to see what he was doing, although she had a pretty good idea and it made her warm inside.

'I'm programming in my numbers.'

His head was bent as she peered around him to watch what he was doing, a little confused about the entire procedure. It wasn't as if she had much experience with the whole casual dating thing. She'd only ever dated Simon.

'This way you'll be able to contact me if there's a problem.'

She was about to ask, *But what if there's not a problem?* when she heard it. Like a bat, she was on Fleur signal. It was a single muffled word. Then nothing for the count of one, two, three, four, five, six… And then the rattle of keys and her front door opening.

Battle stations.

She dived for her clothes on the floor, pulling up tracksuit pants and dragging a fluffy old jumper down over her head, flashing her boobs at him.

'They're back. You have to go,' she babbled, hunting around for his shoes. 'Listen, I'll head them off and get them into the kitchen and you come down and let yourself out.'

She shoved his shoes against his chest. 'Put these on and just stay there.'

Nik was caught by an unexpected wave of tenderness.

'Sybella.' He caught her arm and she gazed up at him with equal measures of annoyance and longing that had him wanting to prolong the moment. 'You are an incredible woman and you shouldn't doubt how sexy you are, or how lucky I feel after last night.'

She looked utterly transfixed, and in that moment he cursed her very young, very stupid dead husband.

Then a voice called out, 'Mummy!'

Sybella said something under her breath and he let her go.

As she came noisily down the stairs Sybella was convinced she had a scarlet 'A' painted on her forehead.

Meg was removing Fleur's coat and scarf. She looked up with a smile.

'I thought I'd bring her home and save you the drive, Syb. I have to be in Middenwold this morning anyway. Mum's having a tooth drilled and she says she can't drive herself home.'

'Mummy!' Fleur ran to hug her and be lifted. Sybella gave a little grunt. Her daughter was getting heavier by the day.

After some kisses Fleur was struggling to be put down. 'I want to show Aunty Meg my new shoes,' she complained, but Sybella had no intention of letting Fleur go up until the coast was clear.

'How about we go and put the kettle on first and make

some porridge?' She charged down the hall, making as much noise as possible. She dived for the radio and turned it up. A cheerful pop song filled the room with chants about love not hurting any more. Fleur began to bop up and down and Meg to dance with her.

By the time Fleur remembered her shoes the porridge had been eaten and at last Sybella was able to step into a shower and wash all of her extraordinary night off her glowing skin.

As she stepped out of the bathroom Meg was examining the broken bedstead Nik had arrayed at the end of the hall.

'How on earth did you do this?'

Fleur appeared with her new red shoes in either hand. 'It must have been the giant.'

A week from the day Nik had climbed out of Sybella's broken bed her name flashed up on his phone with a text.

For a moment he just rubbed his thumb lightly over the screen but purposely didn't read her words, aware of all the times this week he had called up her number only for his thumb to hover and then pass off. Indecision was not his way. He'd let the week get away from him and now he had a choice to make. If he didn't call her they could put a line under it.

He put his phone down to avoid temptation and picked up his drink.

'Problem?' His brother Sasha was watching him.

'Nichevo.'

They were sitting on the deck of his one-hundred-metre yacht, *Phantom*. The great beast was moored in the Adriatic, as it always was at this time of year, off the coast of Montenegro.

The centuries-old ramparts of the town of Budva, with limestone hills rising up behind it, was a starry backdrop of lights as the velvety evening dropped around them. The muted sound of thumping dance music heaved from the other end of the boat.

His brother, although long having given away the drugs and alcohol that had derailed him as an adolescent, seemed to need noise and activity around him. His parties on this boat were legendary. Nik had dropped in via helicopter to spend the evening comparing notes and swapping stories before he headed on to some talks and a symposium in Moscow.

'What are you doing with Deda?' Sasha asked, leaning back in his deckchair, resting his glass of fizz against his jeans-clad thigh.

Bare feet, Nik noted, the scorpion tattoo on his left ankle. His own were clad in hand-tooled moccasins stretched out in front of him. Kind of conservative, but he was kind of a conservative guy.

He eyed his phone again, wondering if she had a problem and he was ignoring it.

'When are you moving him out of that old pile?'

'I'm not.'

Sasha looked out across the water, in profile a muscle clearly leaping in his jaw. His brother liked to pretend he was chilled about everything that went down with Deda, but Nik knew better. He had missed those early years with their grandparents, forced to live with his mother abroad, and it made him diffident about interfering in the old man's life.

He saw himself as an outsider, the irony being Nik knew himself to be the one who didn't belong.

'He's happy with the public prowling around the place. To be honest it appears to have given him a second lease of life.'

'Looks like you're stuck with Mouldy Towers for the interim.'

Nik glanced again at his phone.

'What's her name?' Sasha asked, lifting his glass of fizz and ice to his lips. 'The woman whose call you don't know whether to take.'

Nik debated for a moment saying nothing. 'Her name's Sybella. She volunteers at the Hall.'

'So put it through to your office in London.'

Nik shook his head slightly. 'I slept with her.'

Sasha laughed out loud. 'Does that qualify as *droit de seigneur*?'

'*Nyet*, it means it's complicated.' Nik flashed his brother a quelling look.

'It's always complicated, man. Women as a species aren't happy unless they're raiding your head for what you're thinking at any given moment and then using it to crucify you.'

'Bad break-up with what's-her-name?'

'Just brotherly advice. I've never met a woman who didn't want full access to both your bank account and your darkest secrets.'

'Not Sybella.' Nik settled back, still nursing his phone. 'She mainly wants to keep the Hall open and for me to spend more time with Deda.'

'Oh, man, that's worse. She's already managing you.'

Nik frowned. 'It's not like that. It's complicated because she's got a daughter.'

'So? Has she got a nanny for the kid?'

'Even if she had the money for help it's not that kind of set-up. She's hands-on, home schools, community oriented. She's the whole package.' Nik shook his head slightly. 'Why am I telling you this?'

'So I'll talk you out of it. How long have you known her?'

'Forty-eight hours.'

Sasha obviously did his best to keep a straight face. 'That long?'

It had been enough time to get her life story, lose himself in the wonderland of her body for one night and find himself here on the deck of a yacht half a world away unable to stop thinking about her.

He downed his whisky.

'Why don't you stop overthinking it and show her a good time? You might find out she's more than happy to have a bit of a break from her packaged life. Is the kid's father in the picture?'

'She's a widow.'

'Then I don't see your problem. But if it bothers you that much move on. I've got a phone full of numbers I don't want. I can hook you up.'

'Really?' Nik raised a brow. 'You're farming out women now? Nice, Sasha.'

He ignored his brother, whose personal life was a car crash of beautiful girls and a man who walked away from the wreckage without a scratch, and stared meditatively at the tough glass, stainless steel and tiny circuit board he held in his hand that had revolutionised people's lives and made it hard for a guy to go to ground.

Surely he was doing the right thing keeping away?

He'd seen the photo on her bedside table, of the dark-haired, homely young man with an even younger, bright-eyed Sybella welded to his side.

That was what she needed. A man who would be there for her every day, not one who couldn't fix anyone's life.

He'd tried with his grandfather, but there was no bringing Baba back, which was all Deda really wanted, and Sasha was never going to forgive him for having the upbringing that was stolen from him.

Although Simon Parminter hadn't been there for Sybella in the end, he'd left her pregnant and with some hangups about her body that made Nik wish he could have set the guy straight.

Which was idiotic. If her husband was still alive Sybella wouldn't have looked twice at him.

She was that kind of woman.

Clearly her husband hadn't left her with much money either, given she was leasing the cottage.

He frowned. He could at least stop her payments. If they were seeing one another she could hardly be paying him rent.

Were they seeing each other?

Not that Sybella would accept any handouts. But he hated the idea of her struggling.

Maybe he could sort out the bed. Start with something basic.

Something solid.

Not a bed he would be occupying. Just a bed.

And under no circumstances was he delivering it himself.

He checked the text.

Can I have a yes or no on whether you're closing west wing down? Syb.

After all that, not a romantic bone in that sentence's body.

He exhaled a snort of amusement. She wasn't pining for him at all. Practical, realistic Sybella.

He texted her back.

No, dushka.

No, dushka?

Sybella stood at her kitchen sink, scowling at the message on her phone.

It had been a week since Nik had stormed into her world and made love to her so thoroughly and tenderly he'd set the bar ridiculously high for any other intimate relationship she might have one day, far into the future, and left her with a broken bed and a bit of a bruised heart because *she really liked him.*

Then she'd sent a text.

She'd been sitting in front of an old film last night, sipping on a glass of red and nibbling some comfort chocolate, when she'd worked up the nerve to text him. Not *Why haven't you called?* but a perfectly reasonable professional enquiry. She'd sat there while Jimmy Stewart carried a tipsy Katharine Hepburn back to her room, trying not to envisage Nik reading her text and saying *Sybella, who?*

Then *No, dushka* had popped up on her screen. She'd held her breath, feeling he was suddenly in the room with her, waiting for more. Only there was no more.

It answered her question whether she could show a pre-booked school group through the Hall on Thursday, but left her completely in the dark as to whether he was even interested in seeing her again.

She shoved her phone in her back pocket and ran the tap, frowning as her kitchen sink began to fill with dirty water.

Only it wasn't coming from the tap, it was surging back up the drain.

That wasn't good.

Sybella removed her gloves and opened her laptop, which was sitting on the bench where she'd been doing a little Internet surfing earlier this morning. She'd put 'Nikolai Voronov' into the search engine and up had come a few images of him in a suit at various glamorous functions with equally glamorous women clinging to him, and even more of him in hi-vis gear on mine sites. He did know how to rock a hard hat.

Irritably she wiped the screen of Nik Voronov and tapped the more prosaic 'blocked kitchen sink' into the search engine. The reality of her life restored.

She began rifling through the bottom odds-and-ends drawer, pulling out the shiny spanner her father-in-law had given her for just these emergencies.

Why pay a plumber you couldn't afford when you had videos on the Internet?

Inserting herself under the sink, she focused on fitting the head of the spanner to the grip on the pipe joint.

No, she certainly wouldn't be using those numbers he'd programmed into her phone again.

Frankly she didn't need a man in her life. She was a confident, independent woman. Able to clear drains with just a spanner and a bucket.

She repositioned the bucket.

But she didn't have the upper-body strength to turn the wrench.

'Mummy! Mummy!' Fleur's high, sweet voice came floating into the kitchen.

Sybella adjusted her face into something approximating calm and stuck her head up over the bench.

'What is it, sweetheart?'

'Mummy, the giant is standing in our garden again.'

I wish.

'Is he really? What do you think he wants?'

'Come and see!' Fleur urged.

Another time Sybella would have indulged her and played the game, but the man on the screen had moved on to unclogging your bath in the next video, she still hadn't loosened the pipe grip, and she had to meet Catherine in forty minutes.

'It's very cold outside. I think you'd be warmer in your jeans.'

Fleur hitched up her skirt to reveal she was, indeed, wearing her jeans.

Sybella's tension dissolved into a big smile. 'Excellent fashion choice. Now, I need you to go upstairs and make up your backpack. Do you know what you're taking to Gran's?'

'Ebby.'

Ebby was her much sucked-upon cloth doll.

'We're making a dress for her and fixing her eyes.'

Bless Catherine. 'Pack your jumper—the green one. Do you remember which one that is?'

Fleur nodded confidently, which meant anything could end up in there.

'Off you go. I'll be up in a minute to help. Mummy needs to beat a pipe into submission.'

Sybella crawled forward, angling the wrench at a better angle. She could hear the guy on the online instructional video telling her that sometimes a simple plunger would do the job.

She knew where she wanted to stick that plunger…

'You'll break it,' said a deep voice, testosterone wrapped in velvet, that had Sybella's head snapping back and hitting the top of the sink cavity.

'Ouch!'

She crawled out, her heart pounding in an attempt to escape through her chest, and angled a look up…and up.

Oh, blast.

Fleur had been right. There *was* a giant. Only he'd migrated into her kitchen.

CHAPTER TEN

SYBELLA WAS HOLDING a spanner, dressed much as she had been when he'd come here the last time, casually but this time in jeans and a jumper.

But the spanner in her hand, the brown water in her sink, the harried expression on her face gave him the feeling he was seeing Sybella as she really was, those little duck legs she'd spoken about churning around.

He took in the mess and began shedding his jacket.

'What are you doing?'

He took the spanner out of her hand and tossed his jacket onto a chair. 'I'll fix this. You go fix yourself up.'

Sybella just stood there. Had she missed something? Some lost text where he explained why he'd made no contact for a week? Although the ground shifted under her there, because she could surely have texted him something better than a line about the Hall.

And she was so *glad* to see him.

Then she realised she was standing in front of him in an oversized jumper with the neck and head of a giraffe appliquéd on its front.

Yes, she would fix herself up. Immediately.

Nik had retrieved the culprit in the pipe, a plastic figurine about an inch in diameter, had the water draining away and had put through a call to a cleaning service when he realised he wasn't alone.

He turned around. A small dark head was bobbing around the edge of the doorway.

'Hello,' he said.

The head vanished. He waited. Gradually it inched forward again and a pair of big violet-blue eyes in a sweet squarish little face presented itself. The winter-dark hair that had fallen around her face the last time he'd seen her was tied up in bunches.

She was cute as a button.

'Do you remember me?' he said, keeping absolutely still and feeling completely out of his depth. He had no problem facing down angry mining bosses but confronted with a little girl he discovered he had nothing. 'I'm Nik. I'm a friend of your mama's.'

She didn't vanish this time; instead she edged her way into the kitchen, shy as a mouse. She was dressed in a long green skirt that didn't look entirely legit and some sort of long-sleeved yellow top with an appliquéd picture of a horse on it. Apparently the fashion had caught on.

Nik was struck by how little she was, and also that he was a strange man in her house. He reached for something to say that wouldn't scare her.

She beat him to it. 'You're not a real giant, are you? Because you can fit in a house.'

This was said in a piping voice with a great deal more confidence than he'd expected from her entrance.

'No, I'm not a giant,' he said slowly, trying not to smile.

'Mummy said you were an angry giant and a north god.'

A north what?

'I wasn't really angry with your mama. I got some things wrong. I'm sorry if I upset her.'

She lifted and dropped her small shoulders. 'That's okay.'

Nik remembered what he had in his hand and held it out to her. 'I think this might belong to you.'

The little girl trotted forward and put up her hand to take it. Nik didn't have much experience with kids—in his circle of friends only one had offspring and it was still a baby. He was struck by how tiny her hand was, how perfect her grubby little chewed-down nails. Her eyes were full of curiosity and liveliness and if she was shy it was leaving her fast.

She studied the figurine with the same interest she'd given to him and now seemed to forget he was there.

Nik heard the truck pull up.

He headed for the front door, yanked it open. Excellent. Edbury village might be full of crackpots and run on its own Brigadoon-style timescale, but money talked in London and one of the city's premier furnishing companies had delivered.

Which was when Nik became aware of a rabbit loping past him and out into the garden.

Hadn't Sybella referred to them as house rabbits?

He managed to corral the other one, closing the front door behind him. It took off in a flash into the sitting room.

Which was when her little girl appeared, said dramatically, 'You've done it now,' and disappeared after the fleeing rabbit. Then he heard Sybella shouting from an upstairs window.

.

One of the famous trucks from Newman and Sons with its distinctive gold lettering was pulled up in front of her house.

Sybella watched on in astonishment as the two men flung open the back doors of the truck.

As the pieces of a bed frame and then a mattress appeared and were carried piece by piece up her garden path she threw open the window and stuck her head out.

'I think you've got the wrong house!' she called down to them.

When the men ignored her and kept coming she leaned further out.

'Excuse me, lady of the house up here! This isn't my delivery!'

'It's the replacement for your bed.'

Sybella jumped as Nik's deep voice was suddenly right behind her in her bedroom, narrowly missing knocking her head on the window frame.

The scene of their crime.

She clutched her hand towel to her chest like a maiden in a pulp novel, her shower-damp hair hanging over her shoulders, the rest of her encased in a thick bath sheet, anchored under one arm.

'Nik.' It came out with a load of longing she'd rather he didn't hear. She swallowed, revised her plan. The plan she was trying to formulate as he stood there looking more gorgeous than she even remembered. The best she could come up with was, 'I didn't invite you up here!'

'Bit late for that.' He was looking at the bed. 'We'll get that shifted. You might want to get dressed and come down and supervise Fleur. She's trying to catch those damn rabbits. I think I let one out.'

'Oh, Lord!' Sybella dropped the towel—the hand towel, not the bath sheet—and went to hurry past him but he caught her around the waist with those big hands of his.

'One more thing,' he said as she looked up in astonishment, her body instantly melting like an ice cream in the sun under his touch, and he bent his head and kissed her.

A brief but comprehensive exploration of her mouth and then he let her go.

Sybella stuttered for a moment on her feet, not sure whether to tell him off or ask him to do it again, but that was all taken out of her hands when she heard a high-pitched cry from Fleur and she was down those stairs in a flash. Vaguely she was aware Nik wasn't far behind her.

Fleur was standing in the hall, holding Dodge in her arms, his head pushed comfortingly under her chin as Sybella had taught her.

'Mummy, Daisy got out.' She extended an accusatory

finger at the man standing behind her mother. '*He* let her out. She'll be squashed!'

Nik deftly set Sybella aside with the timely utterance, 'Go and put some clothes on,' and strode down the hall, clearly a man with a purpose.

Sybella sent Fleur into the kitchen to put Dodge in his hutch, grabbed her raincoat, shoved her feet into her galoshes and ran outside, doubting Nik was going to have much luck. She passed the two men carrying a quilted bed end. They stared at her with her bath sheet clearly visible under the semi-transparent plastic. She looked at the bed end, a little baffled by what she was supposed to do. She didn't want Nik buying her a new bed! But at the same time she was currently sleeping on a mattress on the floor and she had a frightened female rabbit to corral.

Sure enough, Daisy had hopped into the compost, long brown ears quivering.

Good girl, thought Sybella, making sure the bath sheet was secure with one arm, scooping Daisy out with the other. At least one of the females around here had some sense.

She carried her back to the kitchen and made sure the hutch was firmly latched. She could hear thumping overhead, which meant someone was in her bedroom. Just what she needed. A man-free zone since they'd arrived here six years ago and now she had them coming down the drainpipe.

She shivered in her towel and plastic raincoat. She really needed to put some clothes on!

Fleur was jumping up and down excitedly in the doorway. 'They've taken away the old mattress, Mummy!'

Sybella tried to access her own hallway but there were three men and Nik and a new mattress wrapped in plastic.

Which was when Nik came up beside her, put a hand to her waist and angled her out of the way.

'Do you think you can get dressed?' he growled.

'I'd like to. I am aware the delivery men don't know where to look.'

'I think they know exactly where to look. Go and put some clothes on.'

'I would but they're in my bedroom! Nik, listen, I can't accept this.'

'Let me do this for you,' he said for her ears only in that quiet, sexy Russian drawl of his. 'I did break it.'

She found herself a little transfixed by the sound of his voice, the look in his eyes. For a single moment she forgot the fact there were strange men in her house, she was wearing a towel under a raincoat and she had to meet Catherine in twenty minutes...

'Sybella! What on earth?'

Then she remembered, Catherine was meeting them, and it had just got worse.

'My mother-in-law,' she bleated. Then more plaintively, 'I have to get all this cleaned up.'

'I've called a cleaning service,' Nik said, observing the well-groomed older lady standing on the doorstep at the end of the hall.

Sybella blinked. 'I'm sorry?'

'Cleaners are coming. Go and dry your hair, whatever it is you need to do. I'm taking you and your daughter to lunch.'

'What about Grandma?' asked Fleur, looking up at her mother for guidance.

Sybella put a hand to her own temple. 'Catherine's spending the day with us,' she said, looking a little harassed. He could see what was coming. *Maybe this isn't a good idea.*

Nik didn't hesitate at this mere stumbling block. 'Catherine too, then.'

CHAPTER ELEVEN

'I BELIEVE YOU were seen having sexual relations with my daughter-in-law up against a car at the Hall.'

Sybella had taken Fleur off to the facilities, or 'loo' as she called it, leaving him alone with the real Mrs Parminter in the low-beamed, snug confines of The Folly Inn, a pub in Edbury with Civil War origins, according to Sybella, and an impressive wine list that spoke of Edbury's prominence on the Cotswolds tourist trail.

Nik cleared his throat. 'That didn't happen.'

The older woman lifted her wine glass with a faint smile.

'I didn't think it did. Sybella is too tightly wrapped up in the memory of my son.'

Great. He really didn't want to hear about the sainted Simon, who'd given Sybella some ridiculous but deeply felt anxieties about her body and left her with a baby, although he guessed the guy couldn't be blamed for that—he hadn't known a truck was coming for him. But he had brought her to a village with so few career prospects she'd been forced to invade his home. Although, Nik was no longer exercised over that little tweak in fate given it had brought Sybella into his life.

'I wish to God it had though,' Catherine added and tipped back the rest of her wine.

Okay, she now had his full attention.

He waited. He figured the stylish older woman was leading up to something and his input wasn't really needed.

'Why don't you take her away somewhere? Marcus and I can look after Fleur for a week, and you seem rather smitten.'

Smitten? Not a word anyone had ever used about him. He usually got ruthless bastard or ice man.

However, Catherine Parminter had just earned her lunch. Taking Sybella away somewhere—alone—had begun to look like an impossible task from the moment he'd clapped eyes on Fleur in the kitchen, and up until this moment he hadn't fancied his chances separating mother from daughter.

He caught sight of Sybella leading Fleur across the room. Male heads were turning. She looked sensational in a green jersey dress made sexy by the simple act of cinching a fabric belt around her waist. Not that she appeared to be thinking about herself and how she presented; she was obviously too busy keeping an eye on her small daughter.

'I believe I will,' he said, not paying much attention to the smug look that now settled on Catherine Parminter's face.

He stood up as Sybella approached.

'Everything takes double the time,' she said with a smile, 'but we get there eventually.'

Fleur wasn't interested in taking her seat. Nik didn't know much about kids but even he could see she was over-excited by the day's events and actively resisting her mother's attempts to get her seated back at the table.

'I might take Fleur for a ramble along the river,' said Catherine, pushing back her chair noisily. 'Why don't you finish that bottle of Merlot, Syb?'

Sybella gave her mother-in-law a look of outright surprise but Catherine was already moving her granddaughter off and there was nothing else for Sybella to do but sit down.

Nik seated himself and picked up the bottle but she shook her head.

'I don't know what's got into Catherine. She doesn't usually like it when I drink.'

'She thinks it might loosen you up.'

'Sorry—what?'

Nik decided to just put it out there.

'She wants you to get laid.'

'What do you mean?' Then her eyes widened. 'No! She didn't?'

'Apparently you're missing out.'

'I'm not! I mean, that's not true.'

'Obviously,' he drawled complacently.

She flushed and looked away, clearly flustered.

'Although it has been seven days,' he added.

'Try six years,' she said, then her eyes flew to his in dismay; she was clearly aware she'd given far too much away.

Nik was a little unsettled by the rush of male primacy he experienced at this news. She hadn't let on once in those cold blue hours of the morning when he'd been keeping her warm in that creaky, too small double bed that he was the first since her husband.

'Carino!'

Nik had his attention ripped off Sybella at this crucial moment by the too familiar rasp of what was becoming a weight around his neck.

Sybella was so startled for a moment she couldn't get past the blaring thought: *She's even more gorgeous in the flesh.*

Marla Mendez, trailed by a small entourage of equally happy, shiny people, had just upped the charisma wattage between The Folly Inn's snug walls and the spotlight was on their table. Which Marla was suddenly all over.

'Nik, darling, I have travelled into the wilds of rural England to find you. I wanted to see for myself if it was true. You have a house in the English countryside. How utterly *Russian* of you!'

Sybella watched as Nik lounged back in his chair and regarded Marla with the same cool distance he'd shown her when they'd first met. Only there was no gentlemanly rising from his chair. Even when he'd thought she was an interloper he'd held the door for her. It didn't dim Marla's wattage by even a degree.

'I absolutely want to see it. Have you stocked it with a private zoo? Aloyshia has a zoo—it's hysterical.'

'No zoo, Marla.' Nik surveyed the group of people moving over to the bar. Sybella was watching them too, and also keeping her eye on Marla, who hadn't looked at her once. He knew he had to introduce them, but something was crouched in the back of his mind, growling, warning him not to let Marla and what she represented anywhere near his time with Sybella.

The noise level from the bar shifted up a notch. Sybella flinched as one of the crowd dropped a glass and there was some laughter.

'Try and keep the noise level down,' Nik advised. 'This isn't New York. It's a family pub in a small village.'

'How quaint.' Finally Marla's dark eyes dwelt on her for a moment and Sybella realised she might be coming under the 'quaint' umbrella. Well, that was one for the books. Marla Mendez saw her as a threat.

Nik looked unimpressed. 'Why don't your people call me when you get back to New York, Marla, and we'll set something up?'

'Oh, no, you will have dinner with me, Nikolai Voronov. This is non-negotiable. I need your advice. Besides, I want you to show me this house of yours.'

Nik said something sharply in Spanish. Marla responded and then made a gesture at her that Sybella was pretty sure went along the lines of, *Lose the local...come and play with me.*

Sybella didn't know what came over her. But Nik hadn't introduced them, Ms Mendez was being very rude and Nik not much better, and frankly she wasn't going to spend another second sitting here like a gooseberry. She plonked her glass out of the way, leaned across the table, took Nik's face between her hands and kissed him. For a moment as she leaned in she saw his eyes flicker with surprise but he sure as hell kissed her back.

Then she melted back into her seat, straightened her dress and angled up her chin at Marla.

'Nik can't have dinner with you,' she said firmly, and her voice didn't wobble a bit, 'because he's having dinner with me.'

'Marla Mendez,' Nik said, amusement lacing his voice, 'this is Sybella Parminter.'

Nik's belated introduction was hardly necessary. She had all of Marla's attention now. 'Sybella,' Marla said, those dark brown eyes acknowledging her at last. 'I am staying at Lark House. Do you know it?'

'I know of it. It's an estate several miles from here,' Sybella said, looking at Nik. 'The Eastmans own it.'

'Yes, Benedict and Emma,' said Marla. 'They are having a party. You can both come, yes?' Suddenly she was beaming at Sybella as if they were friends.

'No party,' said Nik decisively.

'I'd love to go to a party at Lark House.' Sybella found herself staring down a Famous Woman who didn't have thighs and feeling amazingly good about herself. Certainty was rolling through her and with that came confidence.

There was nothing between Nik and this woman, not even a speck of sexual tension, and Sybella felt oddly freed by it. She wasn't that twenty-two-year-old bride any more, feeling as if she didn't measure up. It was as if she'd cut the cord on the spectre of the other woman who had haunted her brief marriage. Only she suspected now that other woman had been the Sybella who was sitting here now, claiming what she wanted.

She'd never felt able to assert herself with Simon for

fear of losing the place he'd made for her here in Edbury when he'd brought her home as his wife.

Whatever was between her and Nik, it wasn't about this woman thrusting herself into the middle of their intimate conversation.

She and Nik didn't have a problem. They just had an interruption to their lunch.

Phones had appeared stuck up in the air all around the pub, angled to take pictures. Sybella guessed at least as a non-celebrity she'd probably be lopped out of any shots that appeared on the Internet.

'We will have such a good time!' Marla put her hands on her hips and swivelled to face Nik. 'I will let you out of dinner, but invite me down to your yacht in Nice this year for Cannes and I will forgive you.'

'There's always an open invitation.'

As Marla retreated to her table on the far side of the room people actually got up and followed her.

Nik leaned forward, the bored look on his face during Marla's performance replaced by real concern.

'*Prohshu prahshehnyah.* I apologise, Sybella. I didn't know she'd be here.'

'Clearly. She followed you, *darling*, all the way to the wilds of Gloucestershire.'

Nik scanned her face. 'She didn't bother you?'

'No, but she's chomping at the bit to bother you. Luckily you'll let her on your yacht. Even if it is only this big.' She inched her thumb and index finger apart to show him.

Nik was observing her as if she'd turned into some species of wild animal he'd never met with before but fascinated him.

'Do you really want to go to this party?' He was looking at her mouth and Sybella, already stirred up by that kiss and her little flag-raising exercise over this man, could feel her erogenous zones jumping up to meet him.

'The Eastmans own the most beautiful stately home in the county,' she insisted. 'Of course I want to go to that party.'

He leaned forward. 'What would you like to do after the party?'

Right now her thighs were liquid and her nipples tight and she knew exactly what she wanted to do after the party and she guessed he did too.

If she were free to do it she would have dragged him into the coat room and made love to him within earshot of the entire pub. Only, she wasn't free to follow her instincts. Her mother-in-law would be back at any moment with her five-year-old daughter and that kiss was the best she could do with what she had to hand.

Instead she asked, 'What on earth do the two of you have in common?'

'Marla came to me for business advice.' Nik's thick lashes had screened his eyes and he sat back, and Sybella got the feeling he wasn't telling her the entire truth.

'You mine for minerals. She models lingerie. It must have been an interesting conversation.'

He looked almost weary for a moment and Sybella shifted forward. 'What's wrong, Nik?'

'She has a son,' he said unexpectedly, 'a few years older than Fleur, and she pretty much stocks her entourage with her family.' He frowned as if this bothered him. 'I think the two of you would probably get on well—if you could put up with the theatrics.'

'And you can't?' But her feelings softened. Single motherhood wasn't easy—for anyone.

'It's business, Sybella. She wants to design what she models and she has a very savvy designer on her payroll who happens to be her sister. I'm the money. Full stop. I'm expecting to see a tidy profit from this transaction, which interests me much more than seeing Marla socially.'

Nik knew then if he told Sybella about the other woman's impromptu striptease ending with her in his lap, even if it was a week before he drove into Edbury, it wouldn't go down well. Not after the story she'd told him about her husband and another girl.

No, Marla needed to keep her clothes on and to stay at the end of a long boardroom table and Sybella could never know the truth of just what his plans were for this small business venture. To use it and close it.

Because she was looking at him with those clear, frank green-brown eyes, and he knew she wouldn't understand.

He touched his hands to hers.

'What are you thinking, *moya krasvitsa zhenschina*?'

'I imagine being your girlfriend would involve more of this kind of thing, with other contenders for the title.'

Nik stroked the length of her thumb with his. She dropped her gaze to their joined hands.

'There are no other contenders.' He spoke softly, his voice roughened by the crackle of sexual tension in the air.

Meaning she was the one? Sybella guessed she had just declared something when she kissed him in front of, not only Marla Mendez, but the rest of The Folly Inn.

'But I told you once before, I can be an eminently shallow man.' He had lowered his voice. 'Because you do know I'm thinking about that roller-coaster ride from your delicate throat down to your slender ankles, and the place that probably thrills me most is when it reaches the lush promise of your lovely, voluptuous bottom.'

Sybella expelled a hot little breath and wondered if that coat closet idea was completely bonkers.

He put his hand under her chin and lifted it so she had to look at him.

'I flew back from Montenegro to take you to lunch because try as I might I couldn't keep away.'

That awful week of not knowing was suddenly at the forefront of her mind. 'But why did you try?'

They both heard Fleur's voice on the perimeter of their table and Nik raised a brow to signify the reason.

Fleur?

Sybella was suddenly a little confused. He'd kept away because she had responsibilities? Because she had a child?

She tried to pull herself together and look cheerful and composed for her daughter, but her head was pounding with the idea Nik found Fleur a stumbling block to their relationship.

Not that it even was a relationship. At the moment it was all very up in the air.

She tried to focus on what her daughter was saying.

'Mummy, Grandma says after tomorrow the ice rink will be closed. You promised and we never got to go!'

Ice rink? Sybella gave an internal groan. She *had* promised. She was the world's worst mother. 'We'll go next year, poppet.'

Fleur's lower lip trembled.

'Where is this ice rink?' Nik's deep voice had both Parminter girls turning their heads to look at him in surprise.

'Belfort Castle opens a rink every year from November through January,' Sybella explained. 'We missed it last year too.' She turned back to her unhappy daughter. 'Mummy is so sorry, darling.'

'Where is this castle?'

Sybella blinked. 'Half an hour west.'

Why was Nik asking all these questions? Couldn't he see it only gave Fleur more of a platform to agonise over it? But then, he knew nothing about children. He clearly didn't want to know anything about her daughter.

'We can do this now,' he said.

Fleur's quivering lip disappeared under her gapped

front teeth. She gave a tremulous little squeal. 'Mummy, Mummy, please. *Pleeeease.*'

'If your mother's agreeable,' he added, and suddenly Sybella's own platform for agonising collapsed.

He was making an effort. For her daughter.

'I think that would be lovely.' She gazed at him, feeling a lot of stuff that she'd have to shelve for the moment.

'What would be lovely?' asked Catherine as she reached the table.

'Ice-skating, Grandma!' Fleur was looking up at Nik as if he might pull a rabbit out of a hat for her. Sybella was aware she was doing much the same.

'Wonderful.' Catherine sat down, drawing Fleur up onto her knee. 'Will any of this involve Fleur spending some time with Marcus and me tonight while you take Sybella to dinner?'

'Catherine—'

'*Da*, if you would,' Nik interrupted her smoothly. 'I'm taking Sybella to a party.'

CHAPTER TWELVE

THE RINK IN FRONT of Belfort Castle glowed with fairy lights as the afternoon dwindled.

Nik parked the SUV and waited for the girls to organise themselves.

On the drive Fleur, buckled up in the back in her child's seat, chattered nonstop about various skating adventures she'd had. From the sounds of it she was the local Edbury skating queen.

'Great, so she'll be okay on the ice?' Nik queried as they approached the boardwalk where they could sit down and put on their skates.

The ice rink was swarming with couples and family groups.

'Fleur's never been skating,' said Sybella with a small smile.

'Okay, then what was the story about winning the race and her friend tripping up and breaking her wrist?'

'Fleur likes to make things up and they usually involve her friend Xanthe breaking something.' Sybella stood up, getting her balance. 'She has an active imagination. I don't discourage it.'

Fleur was dancing up to them now, wanting her mother to put her skates on.

He circled Sybella and Fleur on the rink, keeping an eye on the other skaters as Fleur continually took spills. For the first time in his life he wasn't entirely sure of his role here, but when Fleur toppled for the umpteenth time he leaned in and scooped her up before her bottom hit the ice.

She looked up at him with those big violet eyes, solemn as a church hymnal at this unexpected development, but as he set her on her feet again she kept hold of his hands and let him glide her along the ice. Sybella glided along behind them, applauding Fleur's achievement at actually staying upright, and exchanged a smile with him.

It didn't take long for Fleur to begin to flag and it was time to take her off the ice. She greeted his suggestion they go in search of hot chocolate happily enough.

They were standing a few yards from where Fleur was lined up to hand over the money to the lady behind the counter when he said without thinking it through, 'Poor guy.'

Sybella was so busy going over what today had held and what it might mean, she was delayed in processing what Nik had said.

'Who?' She looked up at him, aware he'd slid his hand around her waist while she'd been watching Fleur. 'Nik?' She raised her eyes to his.

'Poor guy, your Simon, not getting to enjoy any of this.' He looked into her eyes as he said it and Sybella knew then he wasn't going to tiptoe around the memory of her husband.

Thank God.

'But that doesn't mean you and Fleur can't enjoy it,' he said, proving he understood a great deal more than she was probably comfortable with.

Unaccountably a flood of hot, messy tears hit the backs of Sybella's eyes and scalded her face before she could even think to blink them away, and then she was tucked up in his arms, her face, her whole body out of the elements and safe, warm, protected.

'If it were me,' he said in a deep voice, 'I would want this. I would want the two of you to have this. It's okay to move forward, Sybella.'

She nodded her head resolutely against his chest, relief

making her a little light-headed. Then she tilted up her chin. 'Why are you doing all of this with us?'

He shook his head at the inanity of the question. 'Because you've let me.' Then he fitted his mouth to hers and she felt it to her toes.

When she floated back up to take in air there was a stillness about Nik that warned her something wasn't right. He was looking over her shoulder.

Sybella turned around.

Fleur was looking up at them, clutching her change.

'What are you doing to my mummy?'

Later in the early evening, as she drove her daughter round to her grandparents, Sybella acknowledged Nik had handled her immediate descent into panic mode with considerable sangfroid, keeping his hand firmly around her waist and making Fleur see it was all right for him to show her mother affection.

It wasn't as if Fleur hadn't seen her grandparents being affectionate with one another, or Aunty Meg locked in a kiss with the odd boyfriend, all of which Fleur ignored with the lofty disregard of someone who was five and a half. But it was different when it was her mother.

Sybella understood. What surprised her was Nik had understood it better. He'd also handled it better. She'd underestimated him.

Fleur had picked up on what Nik had told her—*I want to kiss your mama because she's so nice*—and when she'd seen Sybella in her frock and heels tonight she'd confided, 'I think Nik will want to kiss you again, Mummy.'

Sybella couldn't help thinking about her marriage as she drove back home.

If she'd had that time over she might not have come back to Simon, and she certainly wouldn't have married him until she'd felt secure in their relationship. She'd been so young, and maybe that was partly why she'd stayed faithful to his memory, perhaps for too long.

Simon had never not been her friend, but Nik was something more. He was her lover.

Nik's SUV was parked outside her house when she pulled up.

As she walked towards him his eyes told her everything she wanted to hear.

He reached into his pocket and produced a bracelet that slithered through his hand.

'I thought this would look well on you.'

He draped it over her wrist. The stones were small white diamonds. Sybella gave a soft gasp.

'Nik, I can't accept this. Diamonds?'

But he was trying to work the delicate silver catch with his big, blunt fingers and there was something about his lack of response and the concentration of his expression and his complete inability to finish the job that made her heart melt. This man who ran an empire was defeated by a delicate catch on a woman's bracelet. God help her, she didn't want to give it back, not when he was being so genuine.

'Here,' she said, handing him her evening bag, 'let me fix it.'

She carefully gathered both ends between the fingertips of her right hand and slid the catch closed. Then she held up her arm to inspect its beautiful drape to the top of her forearm. It was exquisite.

'You like it?' He asked as if it mattered.

'It's beautiful. I don't know what to say, Nik. No one's ever given me such an expensive gift.' She made a face. 'I shouldn't have mentioned that, should I, the cost?'

'I want you to be yourself, Sybella, and I want you to wear it, if you will.'

She stroked her bracelet and wished she had the courage to stroke his face and kiss him and take him upstairs to her new bed, but her newfound confidence of this afternoon seemed to have deserted her. Instead she took a deep breath.

'Didn't Marla say something about a party?'

Lark House was lit up like Christmas. It was also the closest stately home to Edbury Hall.

The owners were apparently happy to entertain the elusive Russian oligarch who was their nearest neighbour on such short notice.

Sybella loved this house. It had all the charm Edbury Hall did not, but, while it was open to the public for functions, it didn't require the services of the Heritage Trust. It was very much a family home, even if that family consisted of two socialites and their grown-up children and was open to weddings and functions on weekends.

All the lights were on, an assortment of cars filled the drive and were planted in odd positions under the oaks, and there were fairy lights strewn along the paths that led to the back terrace, where the party-goers were a blur of colour behind glass.

It was a freezing night and Sybella huddled in her wool coat as Nik put his arm around her and propelled her up those steps.

She hadn't felt this excited or nervous in years, but as soon as she stepped into the warm conservatory the number of people gave her a welcome feeling of anonymity. She was just one of many women in gorgeous bits of nothing. If anything she felt a little overdressed in her backless, knee-length pink silk georgette frock. But she could feel Nik's hand resting lightly above her waist, against her bare skin, and she felt a renewed surge of confidence.

Everyone wanted to talk to them, and then Nik left her alone with their hostess, Emma Eastman, a former model who had married a celebrity agent and was one of the locals who arrived on weekends and whose food bills for her guests helped keep Edbury's local food producers very happy.

'How can it be that you're local and I've never met you?' Emma asked bluntly.

Sybella considered mentioning she'd actually applied to Lark House for work experience but decided the wise course was to smile and say, 'It does seem odd.'

'Of course, we're *delighted* to get Nik here. He's so elusive. When Marla said he'd agreed to come we were over the moon.' She leaned close and said sotto voce, 'I have to say, my husband's line of work means I'm always entertaining performers, TV personalities, big egos, but Marla Mendez takes the cake. She just rang Benedict and invited herself.' Emma suddenly pulled a face. 'Oh, heck, have I spoken out of school? Do you know Marla well?'

'I don't know her at all.'

'Ah.' Emma looked around in a covert fashion. 'Well, just a word to the wise—she's not very happy with you. I suspect she thought this weekend was going to play out somewhat differently. Otherwise I doubt we would have got her here.'

Sybella didn't have to ask what Marla imagined might be different.

'You make a fabulous couple,' said Emma, clearly wanting to hear all the details.

'I don't know if couple is the right word. We've only known one another a handful of days.'

Emma's face fell. 'So you don't think you would have any sway with Nik if Benedict and I were to ask him to sponsor our Wells for Africa project? It would mean so much having his name attached, and I think it would go over well, you know, socially if he was seen to be contributing.'

Sybella felt as if she'd suddenly waded out beyond her depth. Her parents-in-law existed on the edges of the county set in the area, but she'd never paid any attention to it. She didn't like snobs—she'd been raised by two. But Emma's entire manner, even if it was a little manufactured, had something engaging underneath it. She seemed like a genuinely nice woman.

'I'm sure he's open to charitable enterprises—you only have to ask him. He's not nearly as ferocious as his reputation.'

Emma beamed at her. 'As soon as we heard he was bringing a local girl with him we knew Edbury Hall must be in safe hands.'

At dinner Nik was monopolised, but again she didn't mind, although it was a little disconcerting when the man sitting beside her slipped his business card under her plate.

'If you could get this to Mr Voronov, and let him know Forester & Bean have represented most of the established families in the area for over a century.'

Sybella politely smiled and went on with her dinner.

Nik sat opposite her, fielding questions from their host about the ecological impact of mining. Nik rolled out a convincing line about his company's determination not to log where it wasn't necessary and his refusal to use chemicals underground. Any mine was a major habitat modification and Voroncor did their best to limit biodiversity issues. But he admitted freely once a mine had gone in, the site would never be the same again.

Some of the other guests were clearly dinner table ecological warriors—rather like herself—but Nik handled them well. He explained Voroncor had posted bonds with all their sites. Once mining ceased the clean-up would not stop until they had proved the reclaimed land was once more productive.

'So you're not just digging holes in the earth and ruining habitat,' she said to Nik as he pulled her out of her chair after dinner.

'I'd be a poor excuse for a human being if I did,' he said, taking her hand. 'Mining isn't for sissies, Sybella.'

'I don't think anyone here is going to mistake you for a sissy, Nik. Do you know everyone here wants a piece of you?'

He had his other hand around her waist now and was leading her into the ballroom.

She had so many questions, but mostly what she wanted to do was be in his arms, far away from all these people.

'I do know every man here is envious of me at this moment.'

He finally held her in his arms as they drifted onto the dance floor and Sybella rested her head against his shoulder.

Envious? Probably not. But right now her heart was wide open and banging like a barn door and she was just waiting for him to come on in.

Because she could have this. Nik didn't seem to be going anywhere and she'd spent the last week pretending to herself it didn't matter if he came back.

All the silly things she'd been telling herself. None of it was true.

'I never get to do this,' she said confidingly, 'put on a beautiful dress and be admired.' She shook her head against his shoulder. 'I don't know why I'm telling you that. You're a man. You wouldn't understand.'

He stroked an invisible strand of hair from the curve of her neck. 'You've denied yourself a great deal, I think,' he said.

'Not any more.' Emboldened, she put a hand to his chest. 'Are you going to make love to me?' She framed the question she'd been longing to ask him all night.

'Is that a question?' His breath brushed her ear tip.

'Just looking for a time line.' Her skin felt hot; her words sounded so bold and sure.

'You think I brought you here to take another look at your beautiful lingerie?'

Sybella's heart skipped a beat. 'I didn't think men noticed those sorts of things.'

'I notice everything about you.'

Sybella swore she could feel his hand at her lower back through the boning of her gown. Impossible, and yet…

'I want you now,' he said against her ear. 'Is that a problem?'

Sybella moved her smooth cheek against his rough jaw. 'No, not at all.'

'But possibly not at a party,' he observed.

Sybella, a little weak with longing, couldn't at this moment see exactly why.

'Surely there's a guest room somewhere?' Then she sighed, because she would never do something like that. 'Oh, Nik, it's a long drive home.'

'It's been a long week,' he said, his mouth warm against her ear. 'I think we can withstand another half-hour in a car.'

She looked into his eyes and saw everything a woman could possibly want to make her feel like the only female in his universe.

His arm came away from her waist but he held onto her other hand and wordlessly he began to lead her across the dance floor towards the exit.

People parted ways to allow them passage. There was nothing subtle about what they were doing, leaving early, and Sybella was thrilled.

An hour later Nik didn't want to move. Sybella was draped across him. She stroked his chest, nuzzled him.

'I missed this,' she said.

'Six years,' he murmured against her sweet-smelling hair. 'It's a long time.'

'No, you.' She raised her pleasure-dazed eyes to his. 'I missed this with you.'

Nik experienced a surge of something he couldn't control. It was a wave of feeling that had him holding onto her. She didn't seem inclined to let him go either.

Every time he touched her it was like a conflagration of the senses. Every time it felt like the best thing that had ever happened to him.

Why were they denying themselves?

Then he remembered a small person who would arrive home in the morning.

He sat up, banging the back of his head on the frame of the backseat of the SUV.

Sybella winced for him and tried to sit up, but she was hampered by the space. He chuckled and she dissolved into helpless giggles. They had got as far as the Linton Way Forest when Nik had pulled the car off the road and into this clearing. It was private, but they could hear any cars going past on the road.

Nik was certain from the outside they would be invisible; the steamed up windows helped with that. Sybella, still in her dress but wondrously dishevelled, her hair falling down and the hem of her dress so high it hinted at the shadowy mystery between her thighs, gazed up at him. He, with his shirt hanging open and his trousers unbuttoned, was trying to make sense of what this woman did to him. They hadn't even made it into Edbury.

He drove them to the cottage and carried her inside. Put her in the shower and then crowded her against the splash back until the water ran cold. Then he wrapped his bigger, warmer body around hers in the new bed.

'I've got a boat moored at a place I own off the coast

of South Africa,' he said. 'Come there with me for a few days, just you and me.'

Sybella looked at him with those clear hazel eyes. He waited for her to say, *No, I won't leave my daughter* but she surprised him with a simple, 'I'd like that.'

No hesitation, no questions. Instead she asked, 'Can we do it soon?'

'I'll make the arrangements.'

She rubbed her cheek against his arm. 'I've never travelled outside the United Kingdom. Does that make me parochial?'

'No, *dushka*, just busy.' His hand stroked her damp hair and she was whisked back to that evening last week when he'd dried her hair with a towel and she'd first begun to let down her guard with him. He'd also just acknowledged how hard she worked.

There was nothing sexier.

Deep inside her a feeling Sybella had never had before began to stir.

'It's good to take a break from real life, yes?' he said, his chest rumbling against her back.

'Yes,' she sighed. Only later would she wonder if this was only that for him, a break from real life? When it felt all too real to her. But she quieted that thought because, after all, it was only a long weekend away.

CHAPTER THIRTEEN

SYBELLA CAME DOWN the stairs into the galley of the boat, her long bare legs appearing first and then her body clad in a black bikini, a diaphanous shirt unbuttoned and billowing around her. With her hair pulled back in a ponytail she looked happy and carefree and about twenty.

Lust licked along his veins, but it was mingled with something more lasting, something that went along with seeing her so light-hearted, simply enjoying herself and it had a corresponding effect on his spirit. He felt satisfied. *Da*, satisfied. He had her at last.

'Nik, who is this woman?'

It was then he noticed the magazine she was carrying and wondered which old girlfriend she'd stumbled onto, but then he saw the photograph of the eighteenth-century villa on the lake and he knew.

As she came closer she held out the magazine. 'It's got a feature on a Galina Voronov, a Russian socialite with fashion connections and a very nice villa on the shores of Lake Geneva. All very lah-de-dah. She apparently tried to sue you but that failed. You rate two lines, by the way, neither of them informative. Is she a relative?'

Nik ignored the magazine in favour of sliding one hand over her hip as he brought her in against him, the other expertly turning over pancakes in the skillet.

'Who taught you to do that?' she asked, distracted by his unexpected dexterity in the kitchen.

'Baba, my grandmother. We made *blini* all the time. She made her own jam from her orchard and I would stuff myself on them.'

They had a twenty-person staff on the forty-metre yacht

and their meals were sublime, but for their last day of four blissful days together on the boat Nik had sent their staff ashore and they were completely on their own.

He was making her breakfast. It was bliss.

'I can imagine you as a boy, always getting into trouble because you wanted everything your own way.'

'I might have wanted it but Deda made sure I was kept in check,' he said, but he was smiling as he upended the crepes onto a plate with the rest.

'What about your brother? It can't have been easy for your grandmother with two boys.'

Nik's smile vanished. 'My brother wasn't there.'

'I don't understand.'

'Sasha was living with his mother.'

'They split the two of you up?'

Nik looked grim. 'No, my stepmother split us up. At Alex's funeral she took Sasha by the hand and put him in a car and they drove away and I didn't see him again for ten years.'

Sybella was effectively silenced by that image.

'My reputation rises and falls on those blinis,' Nik said, as if he hadn't just dropped a bombshell. 'Why don't you take them out and I'll bring the coffee? Leave the magazine.'

Sybella put the old magazine down on the bench and put a hand on Nik's arm but he gave her a firm smile that didn't reach his eyes. 'Off you go,' he said.

When he reappeared with a tray, coffees and some condiments she knew he wasn't going to say any more, and it was clear this was a painful subject for him, as well it should be. She didn't want to pry, but suddenly she knew this terrible thing about his boyhood.

'I'm so sorry that happened to you, Nik,' she said as he set the tray down. 'Your grandfather would talk about you as a boy, but not Sasha. I didn't make a connection.'

'Why should you?'

Nik settled down opposite her at the table, all masculine grace in shorts and an open shirt, the brown hair on his body glinting gold after four days in the hot sun. Sybella thought she would never get tired of looking at him.

He sighed, rubbing his unshaven jaw. 'Deda and Baba both tried every legal means possible to bring Sasha home but it was like hitting a brick wall. It took Galina going into rehab for Deda to get custody.'

'Galina? The woman in the magazine, who tried to sue you?'

'The same.'

'What was it you said about rehab?'

'Alcohol. She'd run out of money and options, and Sasha was fifteen and I imagine every time she looked at him she saw how much he hated her. So Sasha came home to my grandparents. He was already six feet tall and carrying a mountain of resentment on those kid shoulders of his.'

Sybella weirdly felt a little sorry for Galina Voronov. From what Nik had said she was clearly a troubled woman, but to have your child look at you and hate you?

'How did your grandparents cope?'

'They got him a psychologist and did everything they could, but it was a rough first year. I was just out of national service and doing a science degree, living at the campus. I came home weekends but he resented me from the start, and we argued a lot. I can't blame him. I got everything that by rights should have been his.'

'What does that mean?'

She had linked her hand with his across the table top, but now that hand closed over hers and he smoothed his broad thumb against the pulse point at her wrist. How that had happened Sybella wasn't sure. It was like when they were in bed and one minute he'd be letting her have her way and the next she was exactly where he wanted her and happy to be there.

Yes, Nik was telling her a painful personal story and she was thinking about how sexually dominant he was.

'Nik? What do you mean everything that by rights should have been his?'

'He is their grandson, I'm the ring-in.'

'Nik, that's a terrible thing to say. I know you don't believe that.'

'*Net*, but I suspect Sasha did.'

He must have seen the look on her face because he squeezed her hand. 'When he was sixteen I took him with me on a geological survey in the Urals. I put him to work helping me out and we started to interact as brothers for the first time in over a decade. He was with me when I first saw the abandoned Vizhny mine and talked about putting some shareholders together and buying it up. Sasha said he wanted in, so when I finally made a bid three years later he fronted up with his life savings. It was a risk, our relationship would have imploded at that point if something had gone wrong but it didn't and it's made both of us rich men.'

Sybella got up and came around and climbed onto his lap and pressed her cheek to his rough one.

'I'm so glad you told me this.'

'It's over now,' he said, appearing more interested in how affectionate she was being than seeking comfort. He was stroking the side of her breast so she was distracted when he added quietly, 'Almost over.'

'Almost over?' She drew back and looked into his eyes quizzically.

'*Nichevo.*' He shook his head and gave her a rueful smile, the fingers of his other hand engaging with the ties holding her bikini top together.

'Stop it.' She fidgeted and began to laugh. 'I told you,

I am not walking around topless on this yacht, Nikolai Voronov.'

By the time she'd restored her modesty and been kissed the blinis were cold and the coffee was tepid and Nik had effectively changed the subject.

It was only when she took some of the plates inside that she saw him binning the magazine.

'Can I ask what the legal matter was about with your stepmother?'

He shrugged. 'It's not a secret, *dushka*. Galina was the daughter of a high-ranking Kremlin *apparatchik*. He pulled strings. She got control of our father's archive of work, films, documentaries. She owned all the rights for twenty years and, if that wasn't bad enough, she effectively locked it away so nobody could see it. He's virtually forgotten now in my country.'

'That's wicked.'

Nik stretched his arms and gave his shoulders a roll, showing off that honed physique she already knew very well. But she also got the impression he was shucking off all the tension that had gathered as their conversation had progressed.

'That's my stepmother,' he observed dryly. 'She's a classic fairy tale villain.'

'Will you ever get it back?'

He scrutinised her through those thick lashes. 'You underestimate me, Sybella. I purchased it for several million US dollars two years ago. We settled out of court. It paid for that very nice villa on Lake Geneva you were admiring.'

Sybella shook her head at the figures involved but mostly the weight Nik must have carried all those years, wanting to restore his father's reputation and unable to do so.

It wasn't just the absence of his brother that had weighted him down but the loss of his father's legacy.

'At least she's out of your lives. Is she out of your lives?'

Nik consulted his watch. 'How about we take the tender to a cove near here and I'll show you some of the sights?'

Sybella was changing into shorts and a T-shirt when she realised Nik had once again very neatly sidestepped her question for the second time.

An afternoon spent ashore, climbing to a lookout with spectacular views of the coast, concluded with a swim at dusk near the boat.

The water was warm and Sybella's legs entangled around his, her hair falling in heavy ropes over her shoulders like the mermaid he'd discovered she was, her arms looped around his neck.

Talking about his brother and his stepmother this morning had brought the two sides of his life dangerously close together.

He didn't want to think about his plans for Galina and the money she'd extorted out of him when he was with Sybella. She made it seem unimportant, and, worse, mean and small. Like a spiteful act she wouldn't recognise him as being capable of.

She bobbed in the water in front of him, holding onto him like her own personal life buoy.

'So have you met him? Your real dad?' She was gazing into his eyes as if daring him to change the subject.

Trust Sybella to be worrying over this.

'I've got a name. I know where he is.'

'And?'

'Helsinki.'

'And?'

'I still haven't done anything about it. I don't know if I ever will. I mean, he has a family, a life. I'm busy.'

He could feel her stroking the back of his neck, treating

him like Fleur or one of those damned rabbits she kept. Only he found he didn't mind because it was Sybella.

'No, you're not. You're just like all of us, a little afraid of what might happen when we let down our guard with other people.'

'Is that what I am, *dushka*?' He tried not to sound too disparaging of her well-meant words.

'You know you are.' She smiled at him as if she knew all his cynical thoughts but didn't believe one of them.

The truth was it was getting harder and harder to hold onto that cynicism when he was around Sybella. Her lashes were wet and sticking around her eyes like a doll's. She was so beautiful it hurt. Did she know how strange it was for him, letting another person into his head like this?

'I've let my guard down with you,' he said, almost as a warning, although to her or to him he wasn't sure.

Her arms tightened around him and he could hear her breathing quicken, the almost ferocious way she hung onto him as if that was all she'd wanted to hear, and it answered a need in him he hadn't known until now existed.

'How lucky you are, to at least have known one dad, and now you have a chance with another,' she said urgently. 'Don't let that chance go by, Nik.'

She meant it, and coming from Sybella with her history it had a great deal of force.

He put his mouth close to her ear. 'How lucky your Simon was, to be first in your heart.'

Sybella's grip tightened. 'He's not first in my heart any more.'

They were flying home to Heathrow in his jet from Cape Town International Airport when Sybella, comfortable in a ridiculously luxurious seat, began to giggle.

Nik, standing over her with two glasses of bubbly, raised an eyebrow.

'What's so funny?'

She looked up, smiling at him. 'One day I'll be telling this story and no one will believe me.'

'What, is it the champagne? I thought you'd appreciate it before you were back in that storybook cottage of yours hiding spirits in the airing cupboard.'

'How do you know about that?'

'Your mother-in-law at the restaurant.'

Sybella rolled her eyes.

'So this is my last taste of luxury?' she queried lightly as she accepted her glass, because suddenly they were bang, smack in the middle of making decisions.

'No, although…' He crouched down in front of her. 'How about I ask you what your plans are for the future?'

'Hugging my daughter and not letting her go for a couple of days,' Sybella admitted honestly.

'I was thinking a little more along the lines of your plans for me.'

He started to smile but he was serious too and she could feel her heart thumping like Dodge's hind legs on the kitchen floor.

She thought of her kitchen at this moment, the menagerie of animals, of Fleur running riot and leading a pack of her little friends up and down the stairs like Napoleon orchestrating his Grande Armée, and tried to picture Nik amidst it all. She failed.

'You won't fit,' she blurted out.

'*Lyubov*, I think we've already tested that out.'

Sybella couldn't help it. She snorted. 'I mean in my kitchen,' she said softly, worryingly.

'I'll build you a bigger one.'

She had a vision of her cottage writ large, squashing all the others in the row and Nik with a big hammer.

As silly as it was, it was also true. He had a way of taking over.

She knew she should be happy; instead she was beginning to panic. It was crazy.

'We'll take it a day at a time,' he told her gravely. 'There's no schedule on this.'

She snorted again. With Nik there was always a schedule. He was the busiest man she knew and she had seen the way his grandfather had jockeyed for his attention.

God knew she wouldn't be here if old Mr Voronov hadn't been driven to desperate means to get his grandson down to Edbury...

Sybella had the odd thought she didn't ever want to be in that position.

Driven to desperate means to get Nik's attention.

She just hoped he could accept she came as a package, and she still wasn't at all sure if Nik understood that.

It had been incredible. The boat, the time together. But it wasn't real life.

'One day at a time, Sybella,' he said, leaning forward until she was drowning in his eyes and all of her worried thoughts were subsumed, and then he was kissing her and nothing else seemed to matter.

They had been home for more than four weeks and Nik had spent most of that time under her thatched roof, although he was officially living at the Hall.

It was a situation that delighted his grandfather and caused no end of gossip in the village.

But Sybella didn't mind the talk, especially as she put her head around the door and watched Nik reading to Fleur. Her daughter was leaning against him on the sofa and had her thumb tucked inside her mouth and was deep inside the Wild Wood. Nik's dark velvet voice lent an exotic charm to the story Sybella knew herself off by heart from listening to his grandfather.

These Voronov men had somehow colonised her daughter's life, and for the better. Nik had made an effort to be around and was currently running his empire with a small staff and a state-of-the-art computer system he had set up at the Hall. Some evenings he could be found pacing into the night across her living room as he argued in a mixture of Russian and English via video conference with various boardrooms around the world. If Fleur wandered in he would break off to help her with some puzzle she had or answer her questions. She was a good girl and knew not to interrupt when people were on the phone, but it gave Sybella enormous satisfaction Nik didn't view her comings and goings in her own home as an interruption to his work.

After dinner, when Fleur had been put to bed and the house locked up and Nik had done his usual round of phone calls and she'd gone over the invoicing for the refurbishment of the gatehouse, they bumped into each other in the bathroom.

Nik was shaving, and she just wanted to be with him as well as wash her face.

She shimmied in between him and the basin. He grinned and she wriggled her bottom teasingly as she wrung the warm face cloth to clean off the remains of her make-up.

'Can you ever see yourself getting married again?'

The question took her off guard.

'I haven't given it much thought,' she said truthfully.

She couldn't help noticing what a good pair they made in the mirror. Because she was tall most men looked her in the eye, but Nik's height and strong frame made her curvy body shape fit him, and she saw what he'd been showing her in bed: that they were a perfect physical match.

She preened a little.

'You didn't like being married?' He drew the razor along his jaw.

'If that's a question about Simon wrapped up with a

bow, I did like being married. I guess I felt safe for the first time in my life.'

Nik stilled and met her eyes in the glass. 'You didn't feel safe before that?'

'I felt alone,' she confessed. 'For so long it was just me, and then Simon picked me up and carted me off to his life in the village with his parents and his sister, and their neighbours and friends accepted me just because I was his wife. It was an amazing time for me. And then, a few months later, he had the accident.'

Nik wrapped an arm around her. He didn't mouth any pointless platitudes.

'Can I tell you something?' she asked.

He looked down into her eyes and Sybella knew she was about to take a jump into the unknown. She hadn't told anyone this.

'I cried for Simon, of course I did, but I remember at the funeral thinking, *I'll have to leave now. I'll have to leave the village.* And somehow that felt worse, that felt like the bigger loss.'

It was an enormous admission and Sybella waited to feel guilty, only she didn't.

'Makes sense. It sounds like when you married Simon, you married the life you needed.'

'Yes, I suppose I did.' She relaxed against him, relieved he understood.

'Of course, thanks to Fleur I never did have to leave Edbury.'

Nik towelled his freshly shaven face and switched out the light.

'When did you find out you were pregnant?'

He followed her across the hallway to her room. The house was quiet but for the usual creaks and groans of age. Fleur's door at the end of the hall was ajar and Sybella could see the red glow of her nightlight.

'The day after the funeral. Meg needed a tampon on the day, and it occurred to me I'd been carrying that little box around in my purse for several weeks. So I did a chemist test and then I went to my doctor and my life changed. Again.'

She climbed into her new bed and he stretched out beside her. 'That's the thing about life—it's constantly surprising you.'

He put out the light and pulled her into his arms.

'I guess the long and the short of it is I got married young because I was alone in the world, but I'm not alone any more. I have a daughter, I have in-laws, I have a whole village.'

'And you have me,' he said, and her body began to hum as he slid his hands over her bare skin and found all the places that made her squirm and gasp and sigh.

She woke some hours later, hot and disturbed after a dream. She couldn't remember the contents, but a kind of anxiousness was knotting her chest and presently she got out of bed and quietly crept downstairs. She took her coat off the coat-rack and, wrapped up in it, stepped out of the back door and into her garden. It was the place where she did her thinking.

Spring would be here soon but it was still bitterly cold at night and she'd only stuffed her feet into her old slippers.

The sky over the Indian ocean had been so high and far-reaching. Here at home the sky was hugger mugger with the low hills, but that sense of snugness and enclosure made her feel safe.

'What are you doing out here by yourself?'

Nik wore a pair of boxer shorts, but if he was cold he didn't show it. His physical similarity to one of those more-than-life-size male sculptures the Italians liked to make in the Renaissance was all too obvious.

'I couldn't sleep.'

He didn't ask her why she'd decided to come out into the vegetable patch.

'Do you want to be by yourself?' His deep voice was pitched low.

There was something about the way he was standing there, not coming any closer, that sent a shiver hightailing down Sybella's spine.

'No, I don't. I don't want to be by myself.'

Before she could move his arms were closing around her from behind and she was washed with the feeling of security and rightness the dream had upended. She'd already begun to take this feeling for granted with Nik.

It was so dangerous. He could hurt her and she didn't know if she'd get over it.

But, Mrs Muir be damned. She couldn't go through her life wondering what might have happened if she hadn't let him in. The idea of keeping her heart locked up and on a high shelf held no appeal.

Sybella knew she'd remember this when she was old and grey and had great-grandchildren who would never believe their granny had once given her heart to a Russian billionaire and sailed the Indian Ocean in his boat, a man who had the world at his fingertips but right now wanted only her, Sybella Frances Parminter, and her wide, womanly arse. All at once she began to giggle.

'What's so funny?'

She looked up, smiling at him. 'One day I'll be telling this story about you and me and standing in a vegetable patch and no one will believe me.'

'Come inside, then.' He scooped her up and carried her back into the house and up the creaking stairs and past Fleur's room with its night light and into the corner bedroom where she had moved in alone, almost six years ago after Simon had died, and spent the first night wide awake, tearless and terrified because of the enormity of facing life alone—that was until her baby had kicked.

Fleur had kicked hard. As if to remind her being alone was no longer her fate.

It was time to stop being afraid and to accept that maybe Nik was her fate too.

Nik looked at the clock. He needed to get up but Sybella was lying partially on top of him, her mermaid hair strewn across his chest.

He eyed the low ceiling above them. If he stood up and extended his hand he could flatten his palm on that ceiling. He frowned. Damn this place was small. Built for pygmies. They needed to move.

Which was when he flipped his gaze from ceiling to woman and he grinned. He knew then he could get used to this very quickly. How in the hell had she pulled him around this far in the span of several weeks?

Only Sybella didn't give him a clue, she continued to rest her angel face in the crook of his shoulder, as if he were more restful for her than a pillow. He shared the sentiment. She was warm and her lavish curves cushioned him perfectly. They complemented one another in more ways than one.

He traced the fine skin beneath the soft arc of her pale lashes and trailed his finger down to the curve of her slightly parted lips. She grew more beautiful to him every day and stirred strong feelings in him he didn't recognise.

Smitten didn't even begin to cover it.

He cared about what she thought of him, and at the moment he had a lot to hide.

It was almost ironic when his phone lit up several minutes later and he palmed it off the bedside table, not surprised to see it was from his assistant.

Pavel worked the mad hours he did.

It was a message about an explosion in the Urals mine.

He left Sybella to sleep because he was accustomed to handling things alone, and only remembered to call her when he was in-flight and she wasn't answering.

He sent a message.

Sybella read the message.

Real life intrudes, accident at mine, no loss of life, I'll ring tonight.

For the next two days she didn't hear from him and consequently found herself up at midnight, boiling tea, standing over the sink and wondering how her bed had got to feel so lonely when he'd been sharing it for only a brief time.

Which was when it occurred to her there would probably be some information about the mine accident on the Internet.

She fired up her laptop and sure enough the screen filled with various links connected to Nik's name, but at the top with an accompanying small image was an article from an infamous British tabloid. *Marla puts raunchy moves on Russian oligarch!*

Sybella just stood there. For a moment all she could think was, *Don't look…don't look.*

But she was clicking and scrolling and, like Bluebeard's wife, once seen, she couldn't forget it.

There was an image of Marla Mendez in tiny black barely there underwear, holding a bottle of champagne. Another of Marla pouring champagne over her breasts, her virtually bared breasts, because the bra was basically there as a frame for the main event. Marla climbing onto some guy's lap. The fourth image was recognisably of Nik, in profile, sitting on a chair with Marla astride him, looking, well, looking…

It was hard to get past all the naked female flesh and *her boyfriend*, but Nik didn't seem to be touching her in any way or engaging with her.

Sybella leaned onto the bench and rested her head in her hands, utterly thrown.

It must have happened before they met.

She had no right to be angry or hurt or reproach him with it.

But, oh.

Her kitchen was dark and quiet around her, disturbed only by the ticking of the clock and one of the rabbits making scraping noises in his litter tray.

Nik phoned her first thing in the morning when she was still groggy.

'Sybella, did you see the photos?'

She sat up, rubbing her eyes still swollen from all her crying. 'Yes, last night. How is it going? Are you making any progress?'

He ignored her question about the mine.

'We were in a boardroom, she took off her clothes and I told her to put them on again. I had no idea it was being filmed.'

Sybella fell forward and touched her forehead to the mattress. *Thank you, God.*

She pitched her voice at exactly the right tone, gentle and amused. 'Nik Voronov, are you explaining yourself to me?'

There was a pause. 'Sounds like it.'

'It's fine. I understand. I didn't think anything of it.'

There was a lingering silence.

'Nik, are you there?'

'You are one incredible woman.'

She bit her lip. She'd got this right.

'I try. Now tell me about what's been going on.'

They talked for twenty minutes, he promised he'd do

his best to be back tomorrow evening to take her to dinner and then he had to go. She stepped under the shower, and if she cried a bit it was because she hadn't slept much last night and she had to take a tour today of a couple of dozen eight-year-old children, and it was stressful, and she missed him. It had nothing to do with Nik having his face pressed into Marla Mendez's breasts.

CHAPTER FOURTEEN

*Marla Mendez in Sex Shocker with
Russian Ice Man!*

SYBELLA STOOD OUTSIDE the Edbury newsagents, her whole attention riveted to the tabloid newspaper front page pinned up alongside other legitimate papers reporting on local and international politics.

As far as she knew Nik was in the Urals, dealing with some labour-hire problems on site in the wake of the explosion and had been for the last three weeks. He'd phoned a couple of times, sent a few texts, one saying he should be back in the UK this weekend and another asking her to check something in person with Gordon about the roof on the Hall.

He hadn't mentioned anything about a *sex shocker*.

'I'm sorry, Sybella,' called Leanne Davis, coming outside. 'Doug insisted we put it up…we're required to display all the newspapers. It's not personal, sweetie.'

'No, no, of course not,' murmured Sybella, unable to rip her attention off the image. They appeared to be coming out of a nightclub, Nik in an open-necked shirt looking well…gorgeous, and Marla Mendez in her usual skin-tight handkerchief.

It didn't make sense, and Sybella had to resist the urge to buy the paper just to find out what it said.

Nik had specifically told her he had not seen Marla Mendez socially.

'It's not true,' she called after Leanne, but it was too late, she'd gone inside.

She found herself half an hour later in her car, parked

across from The Glue Box, the local arts and crafts supply shop that held art classes for under tens, furtively peering at the tiny screen on her phone as she read the tabloid article. It was the usual 'friend of a friend' who said they'd been close for months, that Nik had flown her from Miami, where she was currently working, to his Cape Town compound for a secret tryst. She shut it off in disgust.

Me, he had a secret tryst with me.

But the tabloids weren't interested in single mothers living in the Cotswolds and she could hardly take out a full-page ad in the local paper outing herself as the most recent guest on Nik Voronov's boat!

She had just about convinced herself, as she crossed the road and dodged up the steps of The Glue Box, that it wasn't important and she should rise above it when she was bailed up by two of the mothers, one of whom actually asked, 'Can we expect more stories to come out about your rich boyfriend and other lingerie models?'

Mortified, she somehow resisted grabbing Fleur and running. Sybella made herself speak to the art teacher and gather the information flyers amidst a gaggle of other mothers who she was sure were whispering about her. In the car Fleur showed off the picture she'd done.

'This is Jack and this is the Beanstalk, and this is Nik!'

Sybella studied the drawing, the tiny Jack, the scrawny beanstalk and Nik, taking up half the page and coloured golden as the sun, and she realised what she should have been focused on from the start. Having Nik with them, sleeping under their roof, Fleur saw Nik as an established part of her life.

Clearly a big, important golden part.

Sybella started the engine, gave Fleur a reassuring smile. 'Shall we put it on the fridge when we get home?'

'I want to give it to Nik,' Fleur said, fussing with her container of fruit pieces.

Sybella knew then this morning she'd just been embarrassed, now she had a problem.

Nik found her the next day on her hands and knees in the gatehouse with a handful of other volunteers cleaning up after the builders. There was a flutter of movement and a sudden lull in noise to alert her.

One of the women gave her a nudge and Sybella sat back on her haunches and looked around.

Nik stood in the open doorway, arms folded. King of all he surveys, Sybella thought, putting down her brush and pan and rising to her feet. Despite everything that had gone down in the last few days there was a happy girl inside her doing cartwheels because he was back.

He was back.

The problem was she kept seeing him coming out of that nightclub. How many nightclubs had he been to in the last week?

None, Sybella, because he's been on a mine site. You know that.

'Dushka.'

In a couple of strides he was lifting her as if she weighed nothing and then kissing her. In front of everyone.

Sybella pressed her face close to his shirt front as he lowered her until her feet touched the ground, embarrassed but also incredibly pleased.

'What are you doing here?' she asked.

'I could ask you the same thing.'

'The builders need to be supervised, Nik.'

'This is why I have hired professionals.'

'I know, but the committee want to help. We want to be involved.'

'Cleaning?'

'It's a start.'

He stroked her hair back out of her face. 'Who am I to come between you and a bit of builders' dust?'

For dinner Nik took her to a gorgeous little place in Middenwold she hadn't even known existed, a Tudor dwelling as intimate and charming as she could have wished. Sybella resisted raising the issue about the pictures and tried to enjoy her dinner and the atmosphere and Nik's company.

But something of her low mood must have shown through because they left early. He put an arm around her as he led her back to the car, but nothing would lift this feeling. All the pretending nothing was wrong meant something important had shifted between them.

Nik left her in the car while he went to check on one of the brake lights, which gave her time to check her phone. No messages, but she couldn't help almost compulsively looking at those images again.

The little screen filled with the logo of the same popular British online tabloid she'd seared her eyeballs with a few nights ago. Only this time as she looked at it something struck her she hadn't noticed before.

It looked like a lingerie ad.

Sybella was making faces at it when Nik yanked open his door and brought the night and the familiar scent of his faint cologne and him into the cabin of the SUV.

She breathed him in and it just hurt more.

'What's happened?'

'Nothing.' She held the screen of the phone to her chest, not wanting him to know how vulnerable he'd left her. She felt she had precious few defences remaining against him, she could at least keep this one.

'Sybella, you look like someone died.'

Her eyes flew to his and he cursed. 'Sorry, bad use of language. Is this about those photos?'

'I can't help it. People are sending them to me.' She

looked down. 'Do you remember when you told me you'd never been personally involved with Marla Mendez?'

'Sybella, nothing happened, she ambushed me. I told her to put her clothes back on and I wasn't interested.' He sounded tired, which perversely annoyed her more.

'I know all that, this isn't about me not believing you—but why did you lie to me?'

'This happened before we were together.'

He was right, of course. But, 'My friends, workmates, my family, the whole village are looking at this and I know what they're thinking.'

'Who cares what they think?'

'Not you, obviously.' It just slipped out and she stared at her hands in her lap.

'Sybella,' he said, at least sounding as if he cared, 'I don't like it any more than you do but it is what it is.'

'I don't even understand why you're investing in her company.' It was on the tip of her tongue to ask him to pull out, but she felt as if it was her old insecurities at work. A lot of people probably relied on this project going ahead.

She needed to woman up.

But she couldn't help adding, 'Is this what you like?'

'That's not what this is.'

Something in her kicked. 'I asked you a question,' she said softly.

Nik made one of those frustrated male sounds but he didn't answer her. He was smart enough to know when to keep his mouth shut.

She should have been smart enough to shut hers.

'I guess it's what most men like. Woman in next to nothing writhing around on your lap.' She made a wry face at the little screen before turning it off. 'But the champagne is kind of overkill. No woman I know wants to be thought tacky. Who's she trying to appeal to, women who can afford her lingerie or teenage boys?'

'I have no idea.'

'Well, you should probably get up to speed on that, seeing you're her major investor.'

Nik grunted, but she could feel him watching her as if he was gauging the right time to say something to her. Only Sybella didn't want to hear it. She was afraid to hear it. She just wanted to go home.

'I want you to forget those photos,' he said as he closed her bedroom door. 'Because I'm not a regular in the tabloid press, Sybella. I leave that to my brother.'

Sybella slipped off her shoes and lost about three inches in height. 'Well, that's one blessing, I guess.'

'Give it a week and they'll be onto something else.'

'I guess.'

She was feeling vulnerable, any woman would, but Nik didn't seem to see it that way. But why would he? He came across as the guy who either pulled the sexiest woman in the world or, in his words, turned her down. She was the girl who had to live in a small village where everyone was going to pity her.

'But how would you feel if that was me in my underwear with another man?'

He began to chuckle. 'You?'

A flash of white-hot shame went through her, immediately followed by a huge rush of anger at the unfairness of it all. Because, no, she would be humiliated to see images of herself like that, and only two men had seen her in her underwear. And he knew that. She'd trusted him in the intimacy of their relationship to let him know how special this was for her. And now he was laughing at her?

'That's an entirely improbable scenario,' he said.

'Why? Because I can't get another man?'

He frowned. 'No, because I don't date women who flash their assets for profit on the Internet.'

'Funny, the world now thinks you do.'

Nik sighed. 'If this is about issuing some kind of public statement, you know I can't do that, Sybella. I don't play that game.'

'Well, no,' she said awkwardly, because she agreed with him in principle, 'but what about me?' Her voice went small. 'I'm put in a very difficult position.'

She hated having to say it, hated more that he didn't say it first!

'It's just I have to live here, Nik, and now I'm poor Sybella who can't hold her man.'

'Do people still think that way? I suspect that's more in your head than what's actually going on.' He sounded exasperated.

'Oh.' It came out on a little puff of pain.

'I am sorry,' he said, coming over and drawing her to him, his hands resting possessively around her shoulders. As hard as his words were sometimes, when he touched her he communicated a kind of tender restraint that never failed to move her. 'But do you really care what a few locals are saying about you? If I paid attention to the number of people who cursed me out I'd be a pretty poor businessman.'

'I know, but—'

'No buts.' He began unpinning her hair. She released a shaky sigh and tried to relax and let him do this for her, because she knew her hair was her greatest claim to beauty and he did admire it, but try as she might she kept seeing Marla's dark tide of glossy designer hair swaying over her perfect, lace-framed behind moving away from the camera.

She ducked her head. 'I—I can do that. Just leave it, Nik.'

Nik let her go and she scooted over to her dressing table and sat down to put some space between them.

She didn't know how she was going to climb into that

bed with him, because she kept having flashes of those images behind her eyes and everything about her body felt lumpen and unfamiliar to her.

'Sybella, you know there's nothing in this, don't you?'

She shook her head. 'I trust you, I do, it's just you told me nothing intimate had happened between the two of you, and now the photos exist. Why didn't you just tell me then?'

'Because it was tacky. Because I didn't want you having an excuse to call time on us.'

Sybella opened her mouth to tell him she wouldn't have done that, but the truth was it was the sort of thing she might have reacted badly to. It was only now, after more than a couple of months together, falling asleep in his arms and waking up beside him in the morning, that she felt she truly knew something of him.

'Back then, Sybella, I was just the rich guy who made things happen, remember? You would have gone home and never answered my calls.'

She didn't respond because he was right.

'There won't be any more tacky stories, *dushka*. I've always been far more interested in the bottom line than dating models.'

'The bottom line being women's underwear,' she said, trying to be funny but failing. 'Is there that much money in it?'

'Not really. Frankly, I'm more interested in seeing it fail than succeed.'

'Sorry?'

She met his eyes in the mirror and discovered he was looking at her as if gauging something.

'You want it to fail?' she pressed.

He was silent.

'Nik?'

'One of the investors is Galina Voronov.'

'Oh.' The evil witch in Nik's story. The woman whose child hated her.

'When I told you she took everything, I didn't tell you I had a plan to get it back.'

Sybella suddenly felt as if she'd missed some important facet of this conversation.

'But you have your father's film archive now—you paid for it.'

'*Da*, but now she must pay.'

CHAPTER FIFTEEN

NIK HAD FOLDED his arms and, with his height and the breadth of his shoulders, for a moment Fleur's childish nonsense about a giant in their garden flared once more to life.

'Pay?' she echoed. 'How?'

Nik looked back at her. His eyes were narrowed, his mouth taut and he appeared almost wolfish in this light. 'For her sins, of which there are many.' Then he smiled, although it didn't reach his eyes, and unfolded his arms to put a reassuring hand on her shoulder. 'Don't look so worried, *dushka*, I only want the money.'

Sybella gently dislodged his hand. 'No, you don't. You've got more money than the Bank of England.'

'You know me too well.'

Only she was starting to feel she didn't.

She jerked the chair around. 'What's going on, Nik?'

'Galina has invested all her cash assets in another one of Marla's projects. It's how Marla found her way to me. I'm pulling out of Marla Mendez Lingerie and when that happens all Marla's debt is going to come crashing through like a tsunami and it will swallow up the warehouses Galina's money paid for and as Marla's silent partner she will be responsible for those specific debts too. She'll have to sell the villa on Lake Geneva and the money I gave her will be gone.'

'But what about Ms Mendez?'

'Marla will land on her feet, *dushka*, and I'm not doing anything to her that she hasn't already done to herself. I didn't build that debt.'

'She has a little boy, Nik. This is going to impact on him too.'

'As I said, I didn't build her debt.'

'No, but haven't you agreed to sponsor her—surely you entered into a contract?'

'With everything built in I need to withdraw if I feel compromised.'

Sybella's face must have shown what she was feeling because he said more gently, 'It's business, Sybella. It happens.'

'But—but what about her sister, the one you said is the creative behind the label?'

'She's a woman with real talent. I'll make sure she lands on her feet and is given a new opportunity.'

Sybella couldn't believe what she was hearing. 'Nik, you can't play God with innocent people's lives!'

He began unthreading his tie. 'Short-term pain, Sybella, for long-term satisfaction.'

'Other people's pain, your satisfaction.'

She saw the tension rise in his shoulders. 'None of this satisfies me, Sybella. The only thing that would is if Galina had never come into our lives, but I can't turn back the clock.'

'But you can turn back now. You can change this, Nik.' Sybella stumbled to her feet. 'If you do this thing it makes you as bad as her.'

'Spare me the drama, *dushka*.'

'It's not drama, it's people's lives. Marla has a son, her son has an aunty—you're going to bring all this down on them to retrieve money you don't even need.'

'And as I said, it's not about the money.'

'No, it's something worse,' said Sybella chokily. 'If you do this it changes you. Listen, Nik, that day I came to the Hall to give your grandfather back those letters I overheard the two of you talking. You were being so tender with him, and all my prejudices about you fell away. I thought you were that man, hard on the outside because you've had to be, but with a genuinely good heart and the capacity to love your family.' Her voice got stuck. 'You are that man. Don't let her take that away from you.'

'Who are you talking about?'

'Your stepmother. You're letting your hatred for her twist you into something you're not.'

'And you're being naive, Sybella.' He began yanking at his shirt buttons, and as they gave a couple popped and hit the floor but he ignored them, as if a tailored shirt was like a tissue in terms of loss, and Sybella began to feel entirely too queasy.

He must have sensed her distress because he stopped and turned around, his hands resting on his lean hips, shirt gaping, more beautiful than any Norse god and certainly as dangerous in his power and unpredictability.

She might as well have ripped the page out of a magazine and stuck it on her wall; he couldn't have looked more unreal and out of place.

He didn't belong here. He never had. She'd let the giant into the house and only now was she counting the consequences.

'I'm a businessman and I've done some ruthless things in my time to get where I am.'

Sybella could only shake her head. 'I don't feel like I even know you.'

'Yeah, well, maybe you don't,' he threw back at her, pulling off the rest of his shirt and grabbing a fresh one from his open piece of luggage he'd brought in earlier and obviously intended to live out of. Another reminder none of this was permanent.

'But I'm not wasting any more time arguing over this. You just stick to your storybook world, Sybella.' He speared an assessing look up under those thick brown lashes. 'It suits you. I like you in it. I don't want you in this world. It can be equivocal and dark and you can't handle it.'

Sybella realised he was getting dressed again and that could only mean he was leaving, and that was when she realised what had been niggling at her.

'Is that what happened with your grandfather?'

He just kept buttoning his shirt, head down, profile pure chiselled stone.

'It is, isn't it? He climbed into his own version of a storybook to find peace in his last years, to get away from your anger.'

'Don't even start this, Sybella—'

'You probably can't see it,' she said, fumbling to make sense of concepts she'd just got her first glimpse of, 'you've been living it for so long. Nik, has everything you've done been about getting back at your stepmother?'

'*Da*, I built a multibillion-pound empire to spite Galina. You found me out.'

'No, I think you built your business the same way Mr Voronov found a picture in a book and decided he wanted to live in it. To make you safe.'

Nik shook his head, as if she was being ridiculous. 'I don't fear monsters in the cupboard, Sybella.'

'No, because you've had one living in your head. Nik, can't you see? You'll never get rid of her if you don't let it go.'

'Rid of who?'

Sybella sank onto the bed. 'I blamed myself for years after my parents abandoned me. Because they were my parents, the only ones I knew. Then I met Simon and his wonderful family, and they showed me how the people who love you treat you, and that's when I was able to let my parents go.'

Nik's features softened at the mention of her parents; at least he was listening to her, although he didn't look particularly convinced.

'Your grandfather came to Edbury because he's grieving your grandmother and *you* facilitated that by buying him the Hall, and then when things started happening that you didn't authorise, that you couldn't control, you started making a loud noise and threatening people. You were scary when you came down, Nik. You made all of us uneasy.'

'I was protecting my grandfather.'

'Understood, but there was no threat. It was all you.'

'I seem to remember finding strangers outside my grandfather's home and the house open to the public.'

But Sybella refused to be sidetracked. 'Something you would have known about if you'd talked to your grandfather. Is that what I can look forward to? Are you going to put me in a house, fence me in with staff and make sure I'm snug between the covers of that storybook you think I want to live in?'

'Now you're being ridiculous.'

'Am I? What are you protecting me from? That thing your stepmother is still managing to twist you into? What you've just told me paints you as a cold, amoral man seeking vengeance.'

'*Da*, and that is what I am.'

His eyes were hard as slate. Harder than those diamonds he drilled for. Making her feel real fear for the first time. Because she couldn't be with this man. She didn't know who he was.

She tried one last time. 'You're acting as if you have absolute power over these people. If you ruin Marla Mendez's label, you'll be bringing down stress and hardship on a lot more people than Galina. All she loses is money that wasn't hers to begin with.'

Nik felt something hot shoot through the centre of his brain and in its wake he could feel all the doubts he'd had himself, and ruthlessly crushed one by one as he'd walked this path.

But it was a different thing crushing Sybella's words. He looked at her and remembered the first time he'd seen her in full light. He'd thought she was a Christmas Angel.

He didn't even celebrate Christmas last year.

Sybella lived in a different world where people observed all the family and community gatherings, embraced the tenets of 'what you do affects your neighbour' and because of that you strove to do the right thing.

He even understood, given her past, why these things mattered to her.

He couldn't convince her he was right, and a big part of him didn't want to.

He was starting to wonder why he was even here. He zipped up his holdall.

'The moment Marla's label tanks and she moves on, so do I,' he said flatly. 'I want to hear no more of this, Sybella. It's not your concern. It's business.'

She gave him a stricken look. 'Where are you going?'

'I get the impression you don't want me here tonight, and, after three weeks in a mining camp in the Urals, I've had enough of cold, hard beds.'

The next day, hollow-eyed from lack of sleep Sybella took two tour groups through the west wing of the Hall.

After lunch she went down to the gatehouse, where builders were putting in the new exit door and a ramp for the disabled to bring the tourist centre in line with fire and safety regulations. She chatted with a few of the volunteers, trying to soak up some of their excitement and then headed home in the late afternoon just as the skies opened up.

Nik's SUV was out front when she turned up her street and the initial rush of joy was subsumed by uncertainty. She found herself sitting in her little car with the early spring rain beating down on the roof, wondering if she was ever going to find the courage to go in.

It was a lousy day, in keeping with her mood.

Catherine came out onto the doorstep and waved to her. Blast.

'Darling, Nik's here,' she said as Sybella slid past her, dumping her bags and coat in the hall. 'How is it going at the Hall?'

'We're on schedule to open the visitors' centre at the end of the month.'

Sybella submitted to a hug, then Catherine stage-whispered in her ear, 'Nik's in the kitchen. Fleur's playing with building bricks upstairs with Xanthe Miller. The coast is clear.'

'For what?' Sybella blinked at her mother-in-law.

'I think he wants to ask you something.'

This was also said in an exaggerated stage whisper. Sybella often thought Catherine was wasted in the local theatre group. She needed a bigger stage.

A little part of her lit that wick of hope that nothing—not even abandonment at twelve—had managed to snuff out in Sybella: this hope was that she would find her old, familiar Nik waiting for her and last night had been nothing but a horrible dream.

Nik was sprawled on one of her chairs in the kitchen that somehow looked extra tiny with him on it. His shirt was open at the neck and although he was wearing suit trousers, which meant he had been up in London, he looked a little un-put-together, surprisingly unshaven, which was unlike him. He was thumbing his phone.

Hard at work. On what? More plans to ruin the lives of people he didn't even know.

Sybella tried to crush the condemnatory thought. She really didn't want to fight with him.

'*Dushka*, I've got something to show you.' He patted

his knee as if she were just going to sashay over there and plant her behind down.

Sybella pictured herself doing it, Nik sliding his arm around her waist and kissing her neck and both of them pretending she knew nothing bad about him and they were all going to be fine.

Instead she came closer but not close enough.

With a slightly raised brow in acknowledgement of her decision he shifted to his feet because even being a bastard he was always a gentleman.

He showed her the screen on his phone. 'What do you think?'

It was a photo display of rooms, luxurious, spacious living areas, lots of glass, and several bedrooms that Nik scrolled through at top speed, barely giving her time to see it even if she were interested.

'Why are you looking at real estate?'

'It's an apartment in Petersburg I'm looking at purchasing.'

'Oh. It's very nice.' She wanted to tell him about the visitors' centre and she waited for him to ask.

'Purchasing for us,' he clarified. 'You and me and Fleur.'

Sybella literally rocked back on her heels.

'Why?'

'I want you to move to St Petersburg with me. We'll have no more talk about business. This will be our new start.'

Sybella just stared at him.

'Nik, I can't leave Edbury village. This is Fleur's home. This is my home.'

'It's not as if you won't be coming back—both of us have family here.'

'But I have a job here now too. I mean, the visitors' centre is due to open.' She stumbled over telling him because she'd been so excited and now it had just been rendered less important by Nik's out-of-the-blue decision.

'Great,' he said.

'There's a lot to do, but you've seen the plans. I think it's going to revitalise the village.'

'I'm sure it will.'

'The Heritage Trust have put me up for a local achievement award,' she blurted out, wondering why she needed to tell him that now.

'You've put a lot of work in.'

He was saying all the right things but he was watching her as if waiting for her spiel to be over so he could get back to what mattered. To him and his plans.

'The place will be up and running soon and I'm sure there are plenty of volunteers to take over. Hell, I'll employ people.' He gave her an intense look. 'I want you and Fleur in Pitter with me.'

'Nik, we belong here. My family, my friends, Edbury Hall is here and there won't be any volunteers unless I'm around to organise them.'

Nik was shaking his head. 'It's a job, Sybella. You can be replaced.' And with those few words he broke her heart.

Because as he dismissed her ambitions and small but significant achievement with a few tossed-aside words and voiced her worst fear, she could be replaced, the enchantment fell away and Sybella saw she'd been seeing what she wanted to see, not what was there.

A ruthless, ambitious man who got what he wanted when he wanted it.

'I worked hard to make a life here after Simon's death,' she said, finding it difficult to take a proper breath. 'I want to see Edbury Hall flourish and—and I want Fleur to grow up here, and I'm not coming to St Petersburg with you.'

'Then how does this even begin to work? You've seen

how my schedule's been. It's just not practical, Sybella.'
He sounded so cold and hard and certain.

'No, probably not, and above all let's be practical.' She
couldn't keep the bitterness out of her voice.

Nik shifted on his feet. His size no longer intimidated
her, but she could see he was pressing his advantage as a
big, tough guy who always got his own way.

'Sybella,' he said with finality, 'I have thousands of people who rely on me keeping my business interests turning
over. My working life is in Europe.'

If he hadn't told her about his plans for Marla Mendez's
label, Sybella knew she wouldn't be fighting him so hard
at this point.

If she didn't have Fleur to consider she probably would
have given in. Gone with him. Hoped they could build
something together.

But she knew now what he was capable of, and she
wasn't just planning a future for herself with him, she had
her daughter to think of.

'No one is asking you to change any of that. But you
have to give something, Nik. That's what a relationship
is. Give and take.'

At last that hard shell cracked and she saw some of the
old feeling in him.

'Give? I gave Deda a house to live in when he asked for
it. I have allowed you and on your behalf that lunatic historical society to keep the west wing of the Hall open to
the public against my better judgement. I saw this damn
apartment in St Petersburg and I thought of you. Of us.
What don't I give you?'

'Well, you could start by showing some interest in
something that matters to me,' she said quietly.

He gave her a long, hard look. 'This is what matters to
you—a tourist centre at the Hall?'

'What the Hall means to the people who live here, and

future generations. It's not about me, Nik, it's about living in a community and being a part of something bigger than you.'

He laughed derisively. 'When I came down here in January, I was convinced you had an agenda, that you were advancing some little cause of your own, and here we are, a few months down the track, and it turns out I was right.'

The unfairness of it barrelled into her.

'What cause? To keep the history of my village front and centre, so Edbury has something to be proud of? At least I'm doing this for good reasons, unlike you who thinks he can play God with other people's lives!'

'I knew we'd get back to this eventually.'

'Because it really doesn't matter to you, does it?' She broke down, tears filling her eyes. 'Ruin some strangers financially, shunt Fleur and me halfway across the world from everyone we love so you're not inconvenienced.'

'This isn't about my convenience, Sybella, it's you holding on tight to that dead husband of yours,' he shocked her by saying. 'Only think about how long it's taken you to get this far. Think about how hard you had to work to get it. Take it from me, your precious Simon wasn't thinking about you when he set up practice in a town where the only outlet for your career ambitions is some old pile you don't even have much interest in.'

'How dare you? What exactly are you accusing Simon of?'

He gave her a long hard look and she found herself reliving every tender, sweet moment between them. How she'd come to believe he saw something special in her as she did in him.

'Nothing,' he said tightly, shoving his phone into his back pocket. 'Forget it, Sybella. I wish you well with your activities in the Hall. You've fought hard for it.'

With that he walked out of her life, latching the garden gate behind him.

Her environs shrank back down to normal size and everything went back to being as if he'd never been there. Only a part of Sybella understood there would be no getting over him as she had her parents, and Simon. Because she'd found her true self with Nik, the real Sybella—strong, passionate and brave—who had been there all along, only she would have to be a little braver because she was once more on her own.

CHAPTER SIXTEEN

NIK STOOD ON the perimeter of the mine that had been the foundation of his fortune.

It was so vast and for once he didn't see the wealth it represented, the mastery over nature, the supplier of thousands of jobs. He saw it as what it would be for generations, even if he closed it now. A scar on the land. A reminder of all the destruction Sybella stood in opposition to.

She wanted to restore things, to use over what already existed, to make good on the past by bringing it into the present.

All he did was butcher and destroy the things that had hurt him. Lashing out like the nine-year-old boy he had once been, who had lost everything and wanted somebody to pay.

Anybody.

His stepmother was a convenient monster to slay.

Nik kicked a clod of earth near his boot and watched it spatter a few feet in front of him.

It had been three days since he flew out of the UK.

But not a moment passed when he didn't have the oddest feeling, as if something were screwing down in his chest. He woke in the night, chilled, furious with himself.

Every email his assistant passed on about the Mendez show in Milan next week had him visualising Sybella, the look of sheer devastation in her eyes.

He shouldn't have said what he had about her husband, even if it was true.

She thought he was trying to play God, when really all he was doing was trying to mend what was broken. Although ever since he'd told her his plans that broken thing hadn't seemed all that important. What had taken primacy was trying to fix things with Sybella.

He'd come up with the apartment on the spur of the moment. The look on her face. The way she'd pulled away from him. Her refusal to consider leaving the village. It had all coalesced to push him out, and all he'd heard was, *I came here with Simon. I stay here with Simon. You're not fit to wipe his boots.*

But if he was honest she hadn't said any of that. She'd been over the moon about the visitors' centre in Sybella fashion—quietly pleased, and then a little defiant at his complete lack of response.

No wonder she'd lost it with him.

Did he want her to fit into his life instead of making the adjustments to fit into hers?

He knew what a good, healthy relationship looked like. It was the one Deda and Baba had. It was exactly what Deda had been trying to get through his thick skull when he'd arrived down here in January.

'I've found you a girl.'

When had he started thinking he didn't deserve that? What was it Sybella had said? *'You're letting the hatred twist you into something you're not.'*

But deep down he'd always believed that he was that thing. He'd been fighting with this weapon inside him that told him he wasn't a Voronov, he could do whatever it took to play the world and people like his stepmother at their own game. Only that weapon was currently at his own throat and it probably always had been.

The day he'd left Edbury his brother had rung him. He was in the chapel in the west wing at the Hall and he'd been so frustrated after his argument with Sybella he almost hadn't picked up.

'Nice shot of you and Marla Mendez. Deda is furious.'

'Deda's the least of my worries.'

Nik had looked around the high vaulted ceiling of the chapel where apparently he'd agreed tourists could pay their *kopeck* for the privilege and gawp at the stained glass and the slabs on the ground under his feet, where he'd been told sixteenth-century inhabitants of the Hall were buried.

'He emailed me a photo, you and this woman you're seeing.'

'Sybella.'

'*Da*. You were carrying this cute little kid on your shoulders.'

'Fleur. Hang on, Deda emailed you?'

'Yeah, your Sybella got him up to speed on that. Great tits, by the way.'

Hitting his brother hadn't been going to promote family unity. Besides, he'd been a continent away. 'I'll pretend you didn't say that.'

'So you love her?' Sasha had asked.

Nik hadn't even had to think about it. 'Yeah, I do. I do love her.'

There was a pause. 'Are you going to marry her?'

'She's not very happy with me at the moment.'

'Whatever you've done, man, if she loves you she'll forgive you.'

But Nik knew one thing now as he stood on the perimeter of the road that spiralled down into the dark heart of the Voroncor seam: he had to forgive someone else first.

He needed to make a call and take a flight out to Helsinki tonight.

'What's happening, love? Has business called him away again?' asked Catherine, hovering over her as Sybella dragged out her wellies and Fleur's from the cupboard under the stairs.

It had been a week since Nik had stormed out of her

house. A week of pretending, and Sybella was running out of evasions to satisfy her eagle-eyed mother-in-law.

'I don't know.'

They'd been at the May Day celebrations since dawn and Sybella had brought Fleur home for a nap because it was a long day with fireworks tonight.

Fleur appeared at the top of the stairs.

'Ready to go, darling?'

'You're going for a walk?' Catherine demanded peevishly. 'What if Nik calls? Make sure you take your phone.'

'He's not going to call, Catherine.'

'I'll stay here in case he calls.'

Sybella handed Fleur her boots and then took her mother-in-law's face between her hands. 'Go home, Catherine. I love you to bits but please stop interfering in my love life.'

'I have to,' grumbled Catherine. 'Meg won't let me near hers.'

'I want Gran to come,' said Fleur grumpily, picking up on the adults' mood.

Sybella sagged but Catherine must have seen something in her face and, instead of arguing, she helped Fleur with her boots.

'I will see you tonight, pumpkin, at the fireworks.'

Sybella started feeling awful about her behaviour before she even herded Fleur out of the house. By the time she and Fleur were trudging across the field to the high wold she felt wretched. Catherine was the closest person she had to a mother and the older woman's anxiety over Nik's sudden departure a week earlier and determination to bring them together was only motivated by a desire to see her happy.

'Look, Mummy, pretty!' Fleur had a handful of yellow flowers she'd pulled out of the ground.

'That's called oxlip,' Sybella instructed with a smile, and leant down so Fleur could tuck a piece behind her ear.

As she straightened up she noticed properly for the first time that winter had completely melted away and the countryside was fragrant with wildflowers showing themselves among the new grass.

The village below them gleamed with the local mellow gold stonework that was peculiar to the region and the May sunshine hit the church spire.

From here she could see all the windy yellow roads with their stone walls cutting through the countryside below them and the odd car wending its way.

It wasn't a bad place to be miserable. And maybe Mrs Muir was right: there were all kinds of ways to be happy, and she would have to find a way by herself.

He wasn't coming back. And one day it wouldn't hurt this much.

Then she noticed a dark head bobbing up over the next rise directly before the valley dropped down into the village.

It was Meg.

She was running—well, hobbling, really—and as she closed the space between them Sybella saw why. She was wearing stockings and high heels, which looked odd enough as she picked and wove her way around cow pats and muddy spots. She was also carting something under her arm.

'What are you doing with a laptop up here?'

Meg was panting. Apparently cross-fit classes in a gym did nothing for your ability to run an obstacle course up a Cotswold hill.

She handed the laptop over and Sybella obligingly took it as her sister-in-law bent with her hands on her knees and huffed and puffed to get her breath back.

'You. Will. Thank. Me.' She sucked in a few more breaths and then made a gesture at the laptop. 'Fire it up. I've got something to show you.'

'You know the Internet connection is bad enough in the village. I don't know if we'll get it up here.'

'I broke speed laws to get here. Just open the blinking laptop!'

Sybella settled herself down in the grass and did as she was bid.

Meg had taken off her fancy shoes and was gingerly examining the soles, now sadly scuffed and damp.

'They're on the desktop,' Meg said.

Sybella clicked and the screen filled with two faces, one of them so familiar her throat closed over.

Nik and Marla.

'Why are you showing me these?'

'That was taken at last night's opening of Mendez's fashion label in Milan.'

'It went ahead?'

'That's not the question I expected. Why wouldn't it?'

Sybella noted the space between Nik and Marla was filled by a young boy with a shock of dark hair and soulful brown eyes, perhaps around eight or nine. It must be her son.

She could feel her sister-in-law watching her face with barely constrained glee, and then she forgot all about Meg and her entire attention was welded to Nik, and although she couldn't understand the Italian voice-over, she got a lot out of just watching the camera glide over him as he sat up front with Marla, her son, and all the other VIPs while bored-looking coat hangers strutted down the runway. Only…not all those girls were coat hangers. Several distinctly rounded, curvy girls swept the stage in just enough lace and satin to keep them decent. They looked *amazing*.

Marla Mendez's perfect face filled the frame and she said in English, 'I wanted the girls to fill out my sexier designs. I remember the day I had this exciting idea. I met up with Nik Voronov's fiancée, Sybella Parminter, and I,

Marla, looked at her and saw all the shape I wanted for my line. She is gorgeous. She is an oil painting. She has the boobs and the hips and the thighs. The definition of womanhood.'

Fiancée? Sybella felt Meg nudge her.

'So I have the nymphs, the dryads and the Venuses to embrace all body shapes. We women are many things and I want my line to reflect that.'

'How about off-the-rack pricing?' commented Meg.

Then Nik was answering questions.

He was definitely out of his comfort zone with women's lingerie, but then, given his brother was apparently the main driver of the market, he thought he might as well invest.

This brought laughter and more questions.

Then with a faint smile he said, 'No, I have no interest in living in Milan. I am taking up residency in the UK to be with the woman I love. If she'll have me.'

Sybella was vaguely aware Meg's phone was ringing but she couldn't take her eyes off the screen.

'It's Mum,' said Meg. 'She wants to talk to you.'

Sybella continued to gaze at the screen.

There was a volley of high-pitched squawking from the phone. Meg jumped. 'He's rung! Nik rang your phone. Mum says you have to ring him. She says it's no time to play coy. He's shown his hand.'

'I'm not ringing him.'

'She's not ringing him, Mum. Why *aren't* you ringing him? That's from both of us, by the way.'

Sybella had put down the lid of the laptop and was looking up into the sky. There it was, the definite thwack, thwack, thwack. 'Because he's already here.'

Nik saw the forest first and then the church steeple and finally the village spread out on the cleft of the wold.

His attention wasn't on Edbury Hall itself, but the grounds where tents and bunting had been erected. One of the lawns was covered in cars. Several weeks ago it would have been unimaginable. He'd have closed the lot down.

As the chopper flew over the village he could see the maypole on the green, no longer the solitary needle without a thread he'd seen it as when he'd driven into Edbury for the first time, but festooned with ribbons and encircled by dozens of little girls in white dresses, running happily, and not so happily as one or two took tumbles, and their parents and families and neighbours and school friends cheered them on.

He saw St Mary's Church with its glinting spire and the graveyard running up behind it with the tumble of stone markers, large and small. He saw the mass of forest where he and Sybella had first walked together and he'd fallen so completely under her spell it was astonishing he'd been able to walk without stumbling over his feet.

Then he saw her, out on the hill just as Catherine had told him when he'd rung Sybella's phone. Two small figures, but even at this distance he knew which one was Sybella.

'Take it over to the west,' he told his pilot, Max, and as the chopper came in closer the woman next to her began to jump up and down, waving her arms.

Nik was unstrapped and climbing out, the blades still rotating when he saw her coming towards him.

He didn't know where her friend had gone; he didn't care.

As he strode towards her he could see all the anxiety on her face and it tore strips from his chest.

'You didn't do it,' she said.

He came as close as he dared without touching her.

She was wearing a pretty floral dress and her hair was plaited but there were flowers threaded through it, probably for May Day, and she looked like a pagan goddess of spring in her wellington boots.

'I didn't do it.' He shoved his hands into the pockets of his jacket because it was hard to be this close to her and not touch her.

'Why not?' she asked softly, those hazel eyes as anxious as the first time he'd seen her, when he'd mistaken her for an intruder and been trying to scare her.

'I worked it all out. I kept thinking about what you said, about it twisting me, about how I use money and privilege as a weapon…'

She lowered her head but she didn't argue with him.

'You were right, I've known it for a long time, and I kept justifying it because I was angry.'

'She did a terrible thing, Nik.'

'She did, but that's old anger. Frankly, Sybella, I think I stopped expending all that energy on her when I bought back the archive. I did that for my father, by the way. It was my duty by him and then it was done.'

She shook her head. 'Then who were you angry with?'

'Deda, for taking me in when he didn't have to, and Sasha for holding it against me. But it was all me—neither of them felt that way.' His grey eyes searched her face for understanding. 'And that's when I knew I'd decided to be angry with you.'

'With me?'

'I didn't think you loved me.'

The words sounded like paupers, emptying their sacks to show the rich people how little they had. Nik, who had seemed to have everything—money, power, all the confidence in the world—was opening up his heart to her.

She realised right then and there he saw her as the rich one. The one with the love to give and bestow. Just as she had once seen Simon. But she didn't want to be that person with Nik. Because it was absolutely clear to her now that he loved her, had been trying to tell her for a long time how much he loved her, and she had been deaf.

'Do you remember what you said about being angry with Simon, for the accident, something that couldn't possibly be his fault?' He spoke slowly, as if he might stumble over the difficult words.

'Yes.'

'I know you loved him, Sybella, from the bottom of your heart, because that's who you are. What I worked out since I drove away from your house was why you were angry with me.'

'Because I love you, you silly billy,' she said, as if this were obvious.

He smiled then. That slow breaking dawn of a smile, and that he used it so rarely made her think it was only for her. And she knew now that it was.

'Where have you been?'

'I went to Helsinki and met my biological father.'

Of all the things he'd say she hadn't expected that.

'He's a geologist,' Nik added.

'Of course he is.' Sybella was smiling so broadly her face hurt as she stepped right up to him.

Nik fisted his hands because the urge to touch her was almost impossibly strong but he needed to tell her the whole story first. 'He shook my hand, Sybella, and he didn't ask his billionaire son for a kopeck. That's the kind of man he is.'

'He is your dad, then,' she said softly, 'because if the positions were reversed wouldn't you do the same?' She reached up to smooth back his hair in a gesture he'd seen her use with Fleur. It stopped the breath in his body. 'He must be so proud of you, all you've accomplished.'

'I don't know about that. He was interested in you. Do you mind that I talked about you?'

'It depends what you said.'

'I asked for his advice. I told him I was in love with

this beautiful, brilliant Englishwoman and she had a sweet little girl and she was surrounded by all these people who love her, and I'd stuffed up.'

'You're in love with me?'

Nik swallowed down hard. He wanted more than anything to take her in his arms, especially when she sounded so uncertain, but he had to get through this first. He had to give her that certainty they'd once held between them back.

'He told me thirty-five years ago he'd been in love with my mother but he could see that she loved my father more, and he let her go. He told me if he'd known about me it would have been different, he would have made a different choice. And I thought about that, Sybella. I thought about all the variables in our lives. What if your Simon was still here? What if Deda hadn't found that picture in *Country Life*? And I realised the only element in all of this that I could control was me. I had choices. If I went ahead and punished Galina I would lose you. Because you can't love the man who would do something like that, because of the woman you are, and that's the woman I love. That's the man I want to be for you.'

Sybella wasn't sure how it happened, but she was in his arms and it felt like coming home. Her whole life with its good and its bad had been leading up to this moment.

More than anything she knew now this was what the fates had had in store for her.

All the bad things that could happen to a person had rained down on her and then Fleur was born and her life had taken on new meaning, until this moment when it all made perfect sense.

Embodied in this one, extraordinary man. Who was hers.

'Oh, Nik, I've been so lonely without you,' she confessed in a fractured voice as the tears came. 'I don't care where we live. As long as we're with you it doesn't matter.'

'*Net*, it does matter.' His big hands smoothed over her back possessively. 'I want you and Fleur to be with me and I'll do whatever it takes to make that happen.'

She began to cry in earnest and he held her tighter. For once she was happy to give way to his natural dominance.

'I was so proud of you for going ahead with the show, for not withdrawing the funding.'

He framed her face, wiping away her tears with his thumbs. 'On that front I thought I'd have a lot of explaining to do.'

'No, Meg did that.' She sniffed happily, gulping on all the heady emotion surging through her. 'She explained everything, bless her.' Sybella pressed her temple to his bent one. 'I'm just so happy you're here.'

He dropped down on both knees in front of her and she heard Meg give a very un-Meg-like gasp of excitement some distance away.

'Sybella Frances Parminter, will you marry me?'

Sybella's face lit up with a smile she felt from her toes to her fingertips. 'Yes, of course I will.'

Then she fell to her knees in front of him and wrapped her arms around his neck and kissed him.

'That's my yes,' she said against his mouth, 'in case it wasn't clear.'

Then she kissed him again, and Nik wrapped her up in his arms and breathed freely for the first time since he'd driven out of Edbury.

He had her; he was home.

The four of them made their way down the hill towards the carnival atmosphere of the village.

Fleur on Nik's broad shoulders, Sybella holding his hand, Meg picking her way through the field in her heels.

Sybella's heart was overflowing with all of her blessings. Later in the afternoon when family had been told, impromptu champagne had been drunk, her father-in-law Marcus had taken a walk with Nik from which they'd returned somewhat late, having ended at the pub, only then did Nik propose they go up to the Hall.

It was nearing the four o'clock raffle of celebratory hampers and Nik borrowed a megaphone from the guy who was going to call the prize. He walked out onto the lawn and people started to naturally gravitate towards him.

Sybella took Fleur's hand and his arm came around her.

'For those of you who don't know me, I'm Nikolai Aleksandrovich Voronov. I'm caretaker of this house.'

Sybella beamed at her daughter.

'Edbury Hall is forthwith reopened to the public—not just the west wing, but the entire estate.'

His voice carried over the assembled heads of the small crowd and a small cheer went up, interspersed with plenty of 'it's about time'.

'I'll be taking up residence in Edbury but let me put your minds at rest. I will not be turning the Hall into a compound and setting dogs on trespassers.'

Some of the children laughed but Sybella noted the arrested look on Fleur's face at the mention of a dog. She'd have to head that one off when things were a little more normal and she wasn't feeling so loved up. She looked up at her Norse god and didn't think that would be any time soon.

'And just so it's clear,' Nik said, grinning down at her, 'Sybella and I are getting married.'

At the end of the summer the bells of St Mary's pealed as the happy couple emerged into the glorious sunshine.

Sybella, in an off-the-shoulder gauze and white satin gown, her bridal veil set back on her head, and Nik, in a grey morning suit, came first, and then Fleur and her friend Xanthe swinging their baskets of rose petals, the families and friends of both bride and groom spilling out of the church behind them.

The bride had invited Marla Mendez to the wedding, as long as she brought her young son.

Twelve months along almost to the day Leonid Niko-laievich Voronov came into the world in the beautiful local stone house on the wold Nik had moved them into after the wedding.

Leo was christened in the Russian Orthodox Church in London in the presence of his Russian great-grandfather and his English grandparents, but not his parents as custom dictated. He was again christened in the village of Edbury at St Mary's and was carried in the arms of his proud older sister.

There was high tea at the Hall and the whole village attended.

Old Mr Voronov toasted his great-grandson and announced the Hall was being gifted to the National Trust and he was going to live in the new house on the wold with his grandson and his wife. The house was big enough to fit them all and small enough no one would be lonely.

Afterwards Sybella, holding her new baby to her breast, sat on the terrace in the summer sun, watching Fleur tumbling on the lawn with her friends and the absolutely ridiculously large sheepdog Nik had insisted on buying her when they'd first got married. A year down the track it was growing as big as a pony.

'What are you thinking, *moya lyuba*?' Nik's dark voice ran through her senses like dark chocolate and honey, all the things she'd craved while she was pregnant. He hunkered down beside them, stroking the fine pale quiff of hair that was all Leo currently had on his small head.

'How fortunate we are. How fortunate I am.'

'It was fate,' said Nik, a true Russian.

And Sybella was disposed to believe him.

'Although one thing still haunts me,' he mused.

She angled a curious look at him.

'What if Sasha had been the brother who came down that weekend?'

'I can't say I haven't given it some thought,' she said lightly, rubbing a finger consideringly over his lower lip.

'What did you come up with?' he growled, snapping playfully at her finger.

'Sasha's so friendly, he never would have thrown me down in the snow and shaken me like a rattle and sent me on my way.'

'Did I do all those things?' Nik's eyes kindled with hers. 'Shameful. You can never tell our son.'

'I will. I will tell him, when he's old enough to find the right girl, just so he'll know what to do.'

'He's a Voronov. He doesn't need advice about finding the right girl. It's in our blood. He'll know when the time comes.'

So spoke her alpha male. Sybella smiled indulgently.

'When did you know?' she asked.

'I believe it happened when I took off your ski mask, Rapunzel, and I looked into your eyes, but I definitely knew when I kissed you.'

'Like this?' She stroked his jaw with the backs of her fingers and Nik lost his train of thought, moving his mouth over hers once more, careful not to dislodge their small son, who was fiercely guarding his nourishment.

'Exactly like that, *moya lyubov.*'

She looked into Nik's grey eyes and wondered at the idea she'd ever found them chilly. She cocked her head to one side.

'Did I ever tell you? When we first met I thought you were a bear...'

* * * * *

MILLS & BOON

Coming soon

BOUND TO THE
SICILIAN'S BED
Sharon Kendrick

Rocco was going to kiss her and after everything she'd just
said, Nicole knew she needed to stop him. But suddenly
she found herself governed by a much deeper need than
preserving her sanity, or her pride. A need and a hunger
which swept over her with the speed of a bush fire. As
Rocco's shadowed face lowered towards her she found past
and present fusing, so that for a disconcerting moment she
forgot everything except the urgent hunger in her body.
Because hadn't her Sicilian husband always been able to
do this—to captivate her with the lightest touch and to
tantalise her with that smouldering look of promise? And
hadn't there been many nights since they'd separated when
she'd woken up, still half fuddled with sleep, and found
herself yearning for the taste of his lips on hers just one
more time? And now she had it.

One more time.

She opened her mouth—though afterwards she would
try to convince herself she'd been intending to resist him—
but Rocco used the opportunity to fasten his mouth over
hers in the most perfects of fits. And Nicole felt instantly
helpless—caught up in the powerful snare of a sexual
mastery which wiped out everything else. She gave a gasp
of pleasure because it had been so long since she had done
this.

Since they'd been apart Nicole had felt like a living
statue—as if she were made from marble—as if the flesh

and blood part of her were some kind of half-forgotten dream. Slowly but surely she had withdrawn from the sensual side of her nature, until she'd convinced herself she was dead and unfeeling inside. But here came Rocco to wake her dormant sexuality with nothing more than a single kiss. It was like some stupid fairy story. It was scary and powerful. She didn't *want* to want him, and yet . . .

She wanted him.

Her lips opened wider as his tongue slid inside her mouth—eagerly granting him that intimacy as if preparing the way for another. She began to shiver as his hands started to explore her—rediscovering her body with an impatient hunger, as if it were the first time he'd ever touched her.

'Nicole,' he said unevenly and she'd never heard him say her name like that before.

Her arms were locked behind his neck as again he circled his hips in unmistakable invitation and, somewhere in the back of her mind, Nicole could hear the small voice of reason imploring her to take control of the situation. It was urging her to pull back from him and call a halt to what they were doing. But once again she ignored it. Against the powerful tide of passion, that little voice was drowned out and she allowed pleasure to shimmer over her skin.

Continue reading
BOUND TO THE SICILIAN'S BED
Sharon Kendrick

Available next month
www.millsandboon.co.uk

LET'S TALK

Romance

For exclusive extracts, competitions
and special offers, find us online:

 facebook.com/millsandboon

 @millsandboonuk

 @millsandboon

Or get in touch on 0844 844 1351*

For all the latest titles coming soon, visit
millsandboon.co.uk/nextmonth

Want even more
ROMANCE?

Join our bookclub today!

'Mills & Boon books, the perfect way to escape for an hour or so.'

Miss W. Dyer

'Excellent service, promptly delivered and very good subscription choices.'

Miss A. Pearson

'You get fantastic special offer and the chance to get books before they hit the shops'

Mrs V Hall

Visit millsandbook.co.uk/Bookclub
and save on brand new books.

MILLS & BOON